D0447004

THE
LIMINAL
PEOPLE

WITHDRAWN

THE
LIMINAL
PEOPLE

AYIZE JAMA-EVERETT

A NOVEL

Small Beer Press
Easthampton, MA

This is a work of fiction. All characters and events portrayed
in this book are either fictitious or used fictitiously.

The Liminal People copyright © 2011 by Ayize Jama-Everett. All rights reserved.
theliminalpeople.com

Small Beer Press
150 Pleasant Street #306
Easthampton, MA 01027
www.smallbeerpress.com
www.weightlessbooks.com
info@smallbeerpress.com

Distributed to the trade by Consortium.

Library of Congress Cataloging-in-Publication Data

Library of Congress Cataloging-in-Publication Data

Jama-Everett, Ayize, 1974-
 The liminal people : a novel / Ayize Jama-Everett. -- 1st ed.
    p. cm.
 ISBN 978-1-931520-33-1 (alk. paper) -- ISBN 978-1-931520-36-2 (ebook)
 1. Healers--Fiction. 2. Extrasensory perception--Fiction. 3. Psychological fiction. I. Title.
 PS3610.A426L56 2011
 813'.6--dc22
                               201103967
 First edition 1 2 3 4 5 6 7 8 9

Text set in Minion 12 pt.

This book was printed on 30% PCR recycled paper by C-M Books in Ann Arbor, MI.
Cover by Adam S. Doyle (adamsdoyle.com).

وللہ الحمد ويرجع الى اللہ. فقط الأخطاء هي الأغلام.

Chapter One

Nordeen was right to send me. I feel three heartbeats at the ridges of the ancient crater we're resting in. Snipers. I don't know for sure, but their hearts are tense and their trigger fingers twitchy. As soon as I got out of the car their right eyes all zoomed in on something. If they're not snipers then they're one-eyed caffeine freaks with muscular dystrophy in their fingers. At least they're smart enough to know not to shoot me right away. Their boy, my date, Omar, wants what we have. If it's not in the car and they shoot us, they're shit out of luck.

"Stay in the car, no matter what," I say, leaning into the passenger side of the twelve-year-old Mercedes-Benz that has dragged me to this ancient and massive hole in the ground. The meteor that crashed here centuries ago is as cold as Fou-Fou's response to my command. His steady sub-Saharan heartbeat is the only answer I get from the 240-pound menace. He'll play it smart. Always does. The kid in the back is who I'm really speaking to. Nineteen, can't pee straight, and ready to scrap, the native Moroccan looks more spooked than ready. "Understand?" I bark at him in his native Berber instead of the usual French patois we play with.

"I got your back." He says. His blood pressure is pumping a steady drum and bass beat. His rank breath is stinking up the car. I guess his family had the Third World dental plan: eat for a month or get one of your children's teeth fixed. I know which one his parents chose. Maybe when we're done with all of this, I'll help him.

"Get my back by staying in the fucking car, man. Keep with the package until I call for you. Yes?"

"Yes. Yes. But if that fucker Omar starts anything . . ."

"I'll finish it." I barely get the words out before two heartbeats enter the gully from the opposite side. Before I get up I close my eyes. I envision the three ridge heartbeats. They've been waiting for this a long time. Too long. They're tired. It doesn't take much to nudge them into sleep. It takes a little more effort to put them into the REM state needed so that they'll stay down, so I release the brain's native marijuana, anandamide, into their minds in P-Funk-size quantities. With one person it would have been easy. Three folks, far away, hurt a little. Knew it would. That's why I didn't bother to use my abilities to warm myself up. I've got limits just like everyone else.

I read bodies the way pretentious, East Coast Americans read the *New Yorker*. With a little focus, I can manipulate my body and others' on a molecular level. With a lot of focus, I can push organs and whole biological systems around. But if I do it too much, I get tired and hungry. I've got skills. What I don't have is patience.

"Taggert." Hate the way Omar says my name. Hate the way he slams his fucking door all the time. Hate the way his heart is always skipping like it's lying. Hate the way he smells. Hate his Third World breath as I give him the mandatory three kisses business partners expect in this part of the world. Hate this fucking man.

"You're late."

"Don't be mad, Taggert. These things take time."

"What things?" His heartbeat is as erratic as I expected. He thinks he's got us in a trap. It's not the first time someone has thought that.

"Finances, my friend. We have many investors. Some are not so much forthcoming with the funds as you asked. . . ." His bad English irks me almost as much as this crap-ass play.

2

"I didn't ask for anything. You know who I represent, and he doesn't ask for anything. You don't got the funds, we don't have any drama. We'll take our product back to Maximus and—"

"You are so harsh, Taggert. This is not Marseilles, this is Morocco. You must . . ." I open my jacket quickly and brace myself against the cold mountain air. Omar's new trigger boy is as twitched as my foul-mouth nineteen-year-old. Either that or he really has no idea who I represent; he actually palms his .45. Omar—who has sense enough to know what a bad play that would be—tells him to calm down with a wave of his hand. For my part I just hold up the razor-blade necklace my boss gave me.

"Razor-neck crew," I say in the hill language of the Berbers. "That's who you're dealing with. This ain't the medina. This should be a simple exchange. It's not. I'm not in a position to negotiate and neither are you. So we back out of this. Let our betters talk to each other and make another meet time. That's the smartest play for you."

"Hey, French boy! How about you don't tell me what the smart play is?" Omar shouts like he owns something. I don't know who told him I was from Marseilles, but I've never tried to change his mind. I do know why he's so mad. At five-three he's got the Napoleon complex bad. Anytime anyone tells him what he can't do, it's like setting off a firecracker. I didn't do it on purpose, but I'll be damned if I let some midget with an attitude and nothing but new booty for backup bark at me.

"How about you fuck the dumb shit, you son of a maggot-ridden whore, and make your move. Come on, you want to pull something. Want to try and jack the shipment? Make your play!" I open my arms wide and make a grand circle, inviting the unconscious snipers to take their shots. Halfway through it occurs to me that there might be more than three snipers, or that the new booty might be dumb enough to shoot one of the razor-neck crew in the back even with God knows who still hiding in the car. Luckily, I make my round with no shots fired. Omar's face finally reflects what his pulse has been telling me all along. He's scared shitless. I march up close, a nose hair away, before I start speaking again. At the same time I've increased the pressure on the new booty's bladder three times over. He's afraid to move for pissing himself.

"This is your play, ain't it, Omar? Your bosses don't know anything about this, do they?"

"Can you forgive your brother for—" I crack him on the jaw hard with my fist. Before he reaches the ground my elbow gets a piece in, too. Now that he's pissed himself, the new booty feels totally ineffective, even with the .45 in his hand. Who am I to tell him he's wrong?

"You are not my brother." It's a chore to keep it French. That's how I know I'm mad. I only want to speak English when I'm pissed off. "Don't ever let those words pass your lips again." I look up quickly at the new booty. He almost jumps. "Go get what cash you brought. Now." Less than a minute later, a briefcase with six hundred thousand euros is at my feet and the smell of piss has invaded my nostrils. This guy needs to drink more water.

"So we can do the deal?" Omar asks, still trying to salvage something.

"You're short. For every day we have to wait for full payment, it's ten percent marked on. We hold on to the product until then. If it's over a week, we start selling it off, ten percent at a time, to your competitors, and you still owe for the full amount."

"Taggert." He tries to think of some way to convince me to do something else but then realizes I'm holding all the cards. To reward the comprehension I throw him a handkerchief.

"Your betters won't be mad at you for trying to trick us. That's the name of the game. But it was that you didn't have a Plan B. You might lose a finger or thumb or something because you didn't have a way to cut your losses and just do the damn thing the way it's supposed to be done. Don't take it personal. Just the cost of doing business."

My back's to them and I'm heading to the car. Neither one of them will move on me. Omar is dialing right now, trying to ring in on his snipers. I can "feel" a phone vibrating in one of their pockets now. Doesn't matter. We got the money and held the hashish. Plus we didn't leave any bodies behind. Nordeen will be as happy as he gets.

Chapter Two

I wake to the smell of fish, and I know I'm home. Biya, or Al Hoceima, isn't too far from us, but the underground regiment I live with likes to stay away from there. Most of our business goes through that port, which makes it better to not be seen anywhere near by. I leave Fou-Fou in charge of the money and the kid in charge of the hash. Kif, or hash, in the Rif mountains is like water in the ocean. There's no value in it. Six hundred thousand euros, however, is something most people in Morocco can't even imagine. I don't know if Fou-Fou has ever imagined it, but his heartbeat doesn't change. I trust him to get it to the boss. For the past six years I've been living here. My passport works for Nordeen. In exchange I get a nice, three-bedroom, sky-blue house with a rooftop that overlooks the ocean, and peace. By peace I mean I get enough cash to buy anything I want, a beautiful young girl to clean my apartment twice a week, cooked meals, good friends, and even vacation when I want it. As I ascend my ocean-colored stone steps into my spot I can't help but smile a little bit. This home has been a long time coming. I'm glad that it feels like a place to come home to. I don't have a door. Everyone here knows who I work for. They know who I am. At least they think they do—and even *that* reputation is enough to keep people out. Still, it's a comfort to come home and find a box filled with "supplies' from Spain. It's mostly American comics, chocolate, and books

6

I'd ordered online. I'm already on the roof reading and drinking some tea when I see something that doesn't belong. A voice recorder. The type that records onto chips, with no tape. It's Suleiman's. He's recorded something for me, despite the fact that he lives a two-minute walk away. Suddenly my chocolate doesn't taste so sweet. There's an ugly pit in my stomach. It hurts as it expands. There's only one way to get it to shrink. I have to listen. I don't want to. I can tell already. Fuck.

"I'm calling." I'm gasping for air as I hear the voice. "You said to call if I ever needed you. You said you'd come. You said if I used this number then to not use my name and that you'd find me. Find me. I need you. I need you now."

Yasmine. Damn.

The second person like me I ever met was in college. Her name was Yasmine Petalas. A year older than me, and she was gorgeous. If she ever weighed more than 110 pounds I never saw it or felt it. She stood a good four inches shorter than me but could bring down the house with her lungs. Her British-born, Ugandan mother gave her excellent bronzed skin while some recessive gene from her Greek father gave her deep, red, long, straight hair. I knew her for a year before she even knew my name. When I say I fell in love with her, don't understand it as some fantasy made flesh, or some adolescent reciprocal fascination. I would have died for her. She says she needs help, and if I'm the man I want to be then I'm dropping everything and getting on the first thing steaming out of Biya. But I am not that man. Before I leave, think of leaving, I have to get Nordeen's permission.

Suleiman is Nordeen's right-hand man. He knows Nordeen and I have a special relationship but doesn't know what it's based on. Nordeen likes it that way. Still, I show the man respect by never meeting with the big boss until I clear with Sully first. Otherwise he may think I'm making a play for his spot, which I am most definitely not.

Nordeen is like me. I read bodies but I'm not exactly sure what he can do. I know for sure that he can always tell when someone is lying to him. It's a great talent for an international drug dealer, and a fucking annoying trait in a boss. But even that's not Mr. Maximus's real power.

In comics there's this bit character called the Question. He's got no face, and no powers. He's kind of like a brokeass Batman without the Robin. I like him because of the concept of a man with no face being called the Question. It's good in comics. It's bad in your boss. No one knows where he's from. Not me, not Suleiman or any of the other fifteen people he's got working for him. Maybe Fou-Fou knows, but he's not talking. One night we all got drunk in Segovia and tried to piece together the bits of our mystery leader. All we got was a colossal-sized riddle. He won't leave Morocco anymore, but has bank accounts, which have to be set up in person, in his name in the U.A.E, the Cayman Islands, Scotland, and South Africa. All the royalty of Malaysia sends him birthday cards, all at different times of the year. At least five women claim to be his first daughter, he has no sons, and his grandchildren range in age from six months to thirty-five years old. We've never seen any of his wives. His English, French, and Berber tongues are incredible, but he massacres Arabic as though it were a heathen in the noose of the Lord. Yet he's a devout Muslim. By the end of the night of speculation, I was more fearful of the man than I had ever been before.

"Suleiman." I find him with his family, his wife, and his two children ages three and seven. His tastes lean toward the moderate: not a lot of foreign products in the house aside from the expansive television. Minus the drug running, and Suleiman would be the perfect model for the modern Morocco. I take my shoes off before entering his house and wave my hand at his wife, letting her know it's OK to keep the veil down.

"Taggert, say hello to my children," Suleiman commands. He thinks I'm from London so he speaks with a fake Cockney accent. He wants his children to speak English, so I'm put through this cross-generational farce every time I come by. I hate children. Luckily, I don't have to tolerate them for much longer than it takes Suleiman's wife to make the customary tea. We are left in the kitchen alone.

"Was Omar so bad?" he says, examining the scowl on my face.

"He tried to swindle. The boss will have to talk to his people; don't be surprised if the guy comes up missing," I say in rapid-fire Arabic only to be interrupted by Suleiman's brief but fervent prayer for the idiot's soul. The rumor goes that Suleiman used to be in training a mullah before the boss got a hold of him. "This isn't about that."

I pull out the recorder and slide it back to him. Already erased. Sully looks at it suspiciously, then brings his long-scanning, desert eyes up to meet mine. "You asked me to check it once a month when you first came to us. But we haven't used that safe house for a few months now."

"I'm not mad," I lie. "I just want to know if you played it for anyone else." Has he told Nordeen?

"I've only been home twenty minutes. I haven't even had time to see the Old Man yet," he says slowly.

"If it's OK with you, I'd like to tell him about it myself."

"Can I help?" I forgot that Suleiman likes me. His wife has a hard time bringing babies to term. She's lost more than she has. I lied and told her of a tea that would help. In truth I just worked with her body. That's the only reason they have the three-year-old. Suleiman thinks he owes me for the tea. But I don't delude myself about his loyalties. He *will* check to see if I've told Nordeen.

"If it comes to it, yes. But for now let me see what the boss says."

Chapter Three

Nordeen Maximus lives in the biggest house in the city, the closest to the beach. We can almost see Italy from his roof. Everyone here hangs out on their rooftops looking someplace else: Europe, a ship leaving for the States, or places they can't see. Everyone wants to get away from here. Everyone but Nordeen. He hates the cold air on his naked skin with the vitriol of a mongoose in a cobra's nest. Most people think he's frail because on those rare occasions he leaves the house he's always bundled up in layers of Berber sweaters and jackets. That's the way he likes it, people underestimating him.

I never announce myself in his presence. He hates it. I just walk in to his huge living room and sit in a corner. If he's not talking to someone else he's either watching TV or reading. Interruptions cause this blind irritation to rise in him; even to me they come out of the blue. His heart rate doesn't increase, his breathing remains steady, his eyes don't even twitch. He just yells with a fury my brother could only muster when he was truly afraid. Sometimes I love Nordeen and sometimes I wish he'd just die. I've yet to find a subject that he doesn't know nearly everything about, including myself. But he takes the whole "knowledge is power" thing to phenomenal heights. It doesn't make sense to ask the man for anything without giving something in return. Not if you've grown accustomed to a fully functioning reproductive system, that is. He is brilliant and deadly, a combination often hard to like. But I always respect him.

An Al Hoceima whore plays housewife and offers me tea before scampering into the back room. He's always got a parade of them. As he reclines on his floor pillows with shirt proudly open I can almost see why. I don't know how old he is, but he looks to be able to give the nineteen-year-old a challenge. The tea I use like a prop, downing it quickly and healing my scalded throat before the shock has time to set in. It's the type of subtle move only he'll notice.

"You almost broke Omar's jaw for mentioning your brother," he says in the Rif tongue, and I'm mad. Of course he wants to talk business first. I'm gonna sidestep it, then remember he knows when I'm lying.

"He had three men on a ridge for an ambush." True. I've never told him about my brother.

"You handled them?" A question. Luckily I can answer without lying.

"Put them to sleep right before he came. I needed to give him something to know me by. If I used my . . . thing, in that scenario I'd have to . . ."

"The youngster." He smiles, finally putting down the French fashion magazine he was reading. "How'd he fare?"

"Stupid and young. But followed directions well enough. We'd both appreciate any dental care he could get. Pretty sure the Geneva Conventions outlawed that breath." My boss laughs, and I know I'm not in the doghouse for the arrangement I'd reached with Omar.

"I doubt we'll see Omar again. The deal's gone sour with his people. But the parting gift of the cash was appreciated. Now, what's this recording all about?"

"I'm asking for permission to take the razor off temporarily." I don't dare meet his eyes when I ask. Membership in the razor-neck crew is for life. We all have small nicks and scratches on our breastbones from where the razor scrapes our chest. They're never to be taken off. Even when we're having sex. I'm scared shitless that somehow he knows whenever we even think about trying to take them off.

"Ya'llah." If that's all the mangled Arabic I get in this consultation I might make it out of Morocco. But I know enough of my boss to know that if he ever decides I need to go, it won't be him that'll do it. He owes me too much.

"Tell me about it." He says. Good. Not a question.

"I don't know what it is. Maybe something minor, but I doubt it. In any case, it predates my association with you and the crew. I don't want to track mud through your house." I use French because it sounds prettier. He knows I'm not French and appreciates the sentiment.

"What will you do?"

"Find the sender. Do what I can. Get back to my life here as soon as possible." All truth. I'm not gone yet and already I'm missing my house—my fried-fish dinners every night, tea on Suleiman's porch, fantasies about Fou-Fou's past. All of it. I don't want my world to change. I'm hating Yasmine right now. But she dialed a number I swore she'd never use.

"The one who called. She is like us?" The question I was hoping he wouldn't ask. There's no way out of it.

"Yes." This time I'm looking him in his eyes. Any more questions about Yasmine and I'm out the door and dodging bullets. Nordeen has an unusual obsession with people like us. I've never met anyone else who knows more about people with our type of abilities. I don't want to know how he came to his knowledge. But he's not getting any more from me about Yasmine than the sound of her voice and that she's got power.

"Keep the razor on," he says with no change in his face. "Fou-Fou will give you sixty thousand euros from the take. Call back if you need more." He beckons me close, and I'm scared. I've healed him

12

three times from lethal gunshot wounds. Those were the only times I was allowed to touch him. I keep low, making sure my head is never higher than his. I'm expecting a hand to kiss; his deceptively powerful arms embrace my body. Even so, I still can't see him or feel him like I do everyone else. It's like hugging a ghost.

"Remember, what we have is rare." I realize he's speaking English in that no-accent way he does when he's trying to show me compassion. "People like us tend to stay away from each other." I nod. I'm like a cat being held by a kid known to abuse animals. I can't give him any reason to be pissed at me or he'll kill me. I don't know how he'll do it, but it'll be bloody and sadistic. I know because I've been his instrument for such tortures in the past, waiting in shadows and silence for him to finish an embrace just like this before I struck.

"But before you go"—Nordeen breaks his lips apart in an attempt to smile and reclines back to his pillows—"tell me about your brother."

Fifteen muscles in my back spasm, arguing the pros and cons of flight and fight until I consciously remind my body that neither is truly an option. This is Nordeen at his worst, picking at my scabs. And I've just asked for a favor and been given finance and permission for it. All he requires is a story. By the ancient rules of friendship and service, Nordeen is in his rights to hear the whole story. I'm too tired, physically and emotionally, to think of any way out of this. So I speak the truth.

"My brother was like us," I say and wait for a response. Nordeen takes a drag from a nearby hookah. "Only, he could push things with his mind. Make things move. He was strong with his power but weak in morality. I . . . he was four years older than me. I idolized him. Despite what he did to my family. . . ."

"What did he do?" Nordeen asks with the voice of a sadistic psychotherapist.

"He was a bully. My father couldn't stand against him and wouldn't report to anyone what my brother could do. My mother was sick. Depressed. She spent her days washing down Thorazine and Seconal with gin and tonics. But it wasn't just my parents that suffered. The whole town quietly cowered in front of my brother."

"But you didn't?"

"I did!" I say, realizing I'm way too excited by what I'm saying. "I cowered until he ignored me. Then I tried reintroducing myself into his vision, making myself useful. But I had nothing to offer until the day he 'pushed' me out of the second-story window of our house. I broke my arm, then instinctively healed it. He felt it, felt me use my power, and became interested in me." I pause, hoping it's enough. Another damn drag off his hookah, and he's still waiting for more.

"He let me follow him around for a few years. The understanding was simple: I healed him and only him from whatever hurts his bullying got him, and I would get his discards—money, girls, drugs, whatever. None of that mattered. I . . . he let me hang out with him. His company was the biggest prize. At fifteen, I thought I was on top of the world—"

"Until you healed your mother?" Nordeen interrupts me with a truth I've never told him. I know what it feels like when someone picks up a stray thought from my brain: this is not that. I can't get bogged down wondering how Nordeen knows. He does.

"Yes. It was a tumor resting in her brain, causing pain and confusion. I didn't mean to go against my brother. It was just an instinctual healing once I had cultivated my eyes to see illness. The tumor was the size of a quarter and took five minutes to dissipate. My mother's tongue-lashing afterward took longer."

"She chastised you for being morally weak," Nordeen says looking into the corner of nowhere, eyes now milky white, voice now the sound of a whale's cry. "She was disgusted that her womb could produce such bastards, such powerful creatures incapable of compassion." His voice changes, as does the air in the room. My mother's voice comes from his mouth. "Shut up. You bully. You . . . my mind is finally clear. I don't understand any of this. But I know bad, wrong, when I see it. I could barely see for the pain I was in every half an hour for . . . years. But even in that state I knew evil when I saw it. Your brother is definitely evil. But you are not exempt, Taggert. Do you hear me?"

He waits until I wipe the tears from my face before silently demanding I go on. "She went out on her own for the first time in about ten years that day. My dad, a military man, was at the base. I waited in the dark until my brother got home, the whole time breaking and healing my bones, compacting them to be as dense as they could get. I grew extra layers of skin around my knees, knuckles, neck, anywhere my body thought calluses could grow. I hardened my body. And when my brother came home I set about beating him. I punched and kicked and battered him while he threw every part of the house at me. But as quick as he wounded me, I healed and was back on him. In his final fit of rage he brought the house down on both of us."

"He survived." Nordeen speaks. Knowing, not asking.

"Yes, but it takes a team of specialists to teach him how to tie his shoes each day. I caused permanent brain damage." Nordeen nods, giving me tacit permission to leave. I hear his closing sentiment as I walk through his door.

"People like us tend to stay away from each other for good reason, Taggert."

I'm out the house and I'm still alive. What does it mean? Nothing. Only that he doesn't care if Suleiman knows that he wants me dead. Most likely he'll have Suleiman do the deed. If not him then the stink mouthed kid. Doesn't matter. If they come, I'll feel them. And if they come I'll kill them. I'll have to.

My house feels less secure now. The walls are just as sturdy. There's food in the fridge. I could watch satellite TV if I wanted. The crew got it as a gift for me last year. I try to read comics. I try and smoke the product that keeps us all fed. Nothing. I even think about drinking. I could ride into Al Hoceima and hit one of the hotels. Or one of the local whores, even. It wouldn't be the first time, just something I haven't done in a few years. But alcohol just makes it harder for me to use my power. And whores, now they just make me sad. It's too late to get on the road now, even if I wanted to. And with sixty thousand euros in my pocket, I don't even need to pack. I need to just relax in my home, say good-bye to it. I'll need lots of sleep for whatever comes next, and this is the only place I know I can rest well. So I'll sleep because I won't be back here for a while.

The sun came before I realized the moon had left. All hopes of sleep were dashed by memories. And thanks to Nordeen, my memories of Yasmine were clashing with my memories of my brother. Both people like me, but both rejected me. Maybe both for valid reasons. Maybe my brother rejected me because somewhere he knew our relationship had to come down to some serious sibling rivalry. And maybe Yasmine knew I was a freak all along.

Suleiman calls ten minutes after my girl comes through with some apricots, juice, and nuts for breakfast. He lets me know Fou-Fou just dropped off a cash card for me, along with a set of keys. He's asking where he's supposed to take me. If Nordeen is setting me up, he's doing a lot to make sure I don't suspect it. I tell the right-hand man to grub with his family and then pick me up when he's ready.

We're about twenty minutes away from Europe. But it's a different type of Europe. It's filled with hash and illegal immigrants. I could get to Yasmine that way, but then I'm under the radar and still identifiable as Nordeen's. So I take my breakfast slow and then go to the drawer I never use. The drawer from my past, in the closet. It holds the last Italian suit I ever bought and my American passport, the real one. I put both of them on, and it feels like I'm regressing a good ten years. Yasmine better be in real trouble.

Suleiman enters my house with a pulse that's pounding so hard I'm thinking I'm hearing it with my ears. I can imagine his thought process. Maybe Omar made some deal that required Suleiman's head and maybe I was the one who had to do it. It's that kind of thinking that makes him Nordeen's Number 1.

"How do I look?" I ask, showing him open hands as soon as he comes in. It relaxes him somewhat.

"Like a bullshit Frenchie." He's never seen me in civilian gear. "What's the plan?"

"I've got to catch a flight from Fez."

"And then?" Like I know.

I don't even pretend to sleep until I'm installed on the plane. It's less than an hour flight to Marseilles, but it feels like another planet. Planet Old Life.

Chapter Four

I met this kid once. He was maybe twelve years old. His dad owned the biggest telecommunications network in Mogadishu. Don't laugh; those Africans will kill for wireless, literally. The kid was like me, only he talked to the land. Once his hands were in the dirt he could make things grow: enrich soil, deplete it, whatever he wanted. After I showed him what I could do, we became friends. I asked him one time if he wanted to get out of the Mog. He told me even if his father would let him, he wouldn't leave.

"I will die without this land." He said "this" land like he was talking about the plot directly below him. I was still kind of fucked up at the time over Yasmine, so I just chalked it up to his youth—some kid not wanting to have a new experience of the world. But now, as I'm sitting on this plane, leaving Africa for the first time in five years under my real name, I'm realizing how much I had in common with that kid. I'm afraid I'm going to die on this little journey and never come back. It's the never coming back part that's hitting me more than the dying.

After Yasmine wrote me off I went on this ironic death journey around the world, trying to save as many lives as I could. I didn't put myself in danger's way; I pulled up a chair in front of the death TV and started in on a bowl of cocoa crisps like it was Saturday morning and I was a kid again. At first I went through official channels.

Somewhere, I think I still even have my Red Cross jacket. Wherever medics were being fired upon, that's where I went. And once there I broke the rules and went into the no-fly zones. Shit, if suicide by terrorist bullet didn't get me, this trip shouldn't be so hard.

Strange that it feels the same. When Yasmine left, I was alone again. My parents and I had worked out a nonverbal agreement: they would pay for college and never mention my brother or the house they had to sell, so long as I never came home or asked them for anything. Even after she left, I always filled out Yasmine's name and address in the place marked for next of kin. Working my trick on a young village boy or girl torn up by automatic fire as bullets whiz by me and all I can think about is what Yasmine going to do when she finds herself the proud owner of my headless corpse? Never happened.

I can't say a few bullets didn't catch me, or that my ambulance never hit a stray landmine, but my body has an automatic healing effect. It's autonomic—hell, it happens even faster when I black out. It only took four fatal gunshot wounds to realize that. And I couldn't even get drunk enough to mourn my inability to commit suicide—my body wouldn't let me. So instead I got immoral.

Turns out an EMT is like a street doctor for those who can't afford a hospital visit. As I was about to go back to London from Sri Lanka, an African with a British accent approached me about doing some fieldwork in the Continent. He was looking for field-trained medics unafraid of bullets. And he definitely paid more than the Red Cross. So to Somalia I went, working for a warlord. I ordered enough supplies I didn't need and made sure to not heal anyone too quickly. Still, I got a reputation for being able to handle almost anything after the warlord got cancer in his foot and I "saved" him without chemo. You'd think he'd be appreciative. Instead the bastard started renting me out. First to a Liberian friend of his and then to some Colombians he knew. But the cash was good and I was treated like a king. I liked the life and would've stayed in it if not for the mother who brought her daughter to me one night begging that I heal her. The girl was nine years old and had more herpes sores covering her hairless vagina than zits covering her face. The mother pleaded with me to heal her as she was my warlord's favorite and he didn't know the mother had been renting the girl out to other people. I healed the girl in silence. No tricks, no fake medications, no examination. I just laid my hands on the sides of her head and spent my rage on every cell of that virus in her body. The sores literally fell off of her. And I fell off the planet.

I'm not going to say I was innocent back then. But I knew less of what people were willing to live with, to put up with, to invite, in order to survive than I do now. Had I seen babies turned out as prostitutes before? Of course. Had I seen them ravaged by S.T.I.'s? Most definitely. Had I seen creatures disguised as mothers pimping their kids out previous to that? Yes. But to see it all together, at once, staring at me with hopeful eyes filled with understanding, inviting me to join their compromised way of life, it was too much for a younger me to bear. How was I to know I was just delaying the inevitable?

I figured someone would come for me. I couldn't just walk out of the Mog. But that's what I did. Out of Mogadishu into Kenya up to Ethiopia and then across the Sudan, Chad, and the Niger. My dark skin helped me blend in. Anyone who came at me with guns, I healed. When I needed shelter I healed people for it. The same with food. There are a lot of sick people in Africa. I became a bit of a legend. I never spoke to anyone and never rested more than one day in any place. It took me a year and a half, but I walked from Mogadishu to Bandiagara, Mali. Why there? No idea. The place pulled me to it. The people there, the Dogon, were the only ones that reacted to my healings with absolutely no surprise. I stayed amongst them for a month, learning their language, helping them find a way to eke out a survival in the poorest country in the world, crying about all I had seen . . . before they kicked me out.

"Healers are poison to the warrior soul," the village chiefs told me. "They make us forget the gift of death. This is a hard land, and we must be as hard as it to survive. You are a good man, but you make us soft." Where do you go when dirt farmers don't want you?

It's only after the plane touches down that I realize I actually did fall asleep. Haven't been to Marseilles in a while. Didn't realize the Parisians were buying up vacation spots. I wonder how long it'll be before they own the minarets? Doesn't matter. I'm through customs with my carry-on and American passport with only a little bit of trouble. I have to explain why the last country I was supposed to be in was Sri Lanka and why I'm coming in from Morocco. Too bad the customs agent was taken by fever, cold sweats, blurred vision, and swollen glands, which all got worse the longer he spoke with me.

A cab is easy enough to find, and my French is still passable as native. "The best hotel you can find" is all I say to the driver. He sees the suit and knows I'm not bullshitting. I walk in with my cash card that looks like a credit card and get a suite without a reservation or an explanation. Forty minutes after getting off the plane I'm in a hotel, alone. No Yasmine, no razor-necks, no one. Yup. Another planet.

Chapter Five

I thought I was hard until that Somali girl. I thought I was used to soli-tude until the dirt farmers told me I had to go. I thought I knew what power was until I met Nordeen.

All through my silent trek, I dreamed about what it would be like to have the kid who talked to dirt with me. We could've cut a green healthy veldt through some of the roughest patches of Africa. A few times, after healings mostly, people would try to follow me, even worship me. But I'd keep walking. I'd walk without fear near wild animals or wild people. My followers would suffer the Peter syndrome and betray me three times before my death. Some people shot at me, some people hit. No one ever stopped me. The animals were smarter. They'd try and stalk me but soon they'd realize some-thing was different and, like most of my life, I'd be left alone. Still, the power to walk, to be quiet, and to barely eat or drink for over a year had me focusing on my abilities in a whole new way. In the darkness of African nights, when no one was around, I had to ask myself the uncomfortable question. Was I a God? I still slept and I still ate, but a strange inkling in me questioned the need. If I were stronger, more in tune with my power, like my brother, would I even need those last vestiges of my humanity? It was a question Nordeen had been con-templating since well before my birth.

✳

I first met Suleiman and Fou-Fou in Mauritania. I was wandering north, for the same reason I had spent a year and change wandering west—just 'cause. They came upon me in the middle of nowhere and called me out in the most bizarre way possible.

"My employer says he knows about you. He says for you to know about yourself, you should come with us and meet him." I went to their Jeep and reached for a hand to get in. Both men recoiled.

"With respect," Suleiman said, "my employer also instructed us not to touch you in any way." In its own way my life as a healer prepared me for being treated as a threat, so there were few words between me and the razor-necks until long after I made my first peace with Nordeen.

They drove me out to a clear piece of desert and flagged down a low-flying aircraft. Within a few hours I found myself in a small villa just outside of Marrakech. Creature comforts such as food, water, a bed, and a roof over my head were distant memories. I greeted them like war buddies long thought dead. One luxury I was better without was a mirror. It was as though I had absorbed my patients' illnesses, not cured them. I was pockmarked and blemished from the sun on all the spots of my face that weren't covered by a kinky mat of hair. Whatever pigment, other than rust, that had once colored my eyes seemed to have retired years ago. I examined my body visually for the first time since the Mog and found that I looked like someone who had crossed African cities, savannah, mountaintops, and desert on foot with no supplies. I had feet, and then I had calloused rhino-hide skin between where my feet ended and ground began. If I weighed more than ninety-two pounds it was not due to food. My clothes, before Nordeen's donation of silk pants and a loose-fitting djellabah, were gifted to me by some of the poorest people in one of the poorest nations. Any thoughts of godliness felt like a joke at that moment.

✳

Razor-necks don't operate in Marseilles. Angelwise Crew, the Question Marks, even the Brunfeld Collective, none of them set foot in Marseilles. It's a no-fly zone for scams, deals, anything illegal. Nordeen always had special prohibitions against me coming here. All he'd say about it is that it used to be cursed and now it's protected. That's exactly why I'm here.

I pay my tab with the card then put it in an envelope and mail it to one of our drop houses. It'll take a month before it gets back to him. No way in hell he's not tracking every purchase, every cash withdrawal on it. Wouldn't expect any less of him. But I've got to handle this on my own. And the boss has a way of making things more . . . difficult than they need to be.

So I ditch the hotel, burning the credit card for sure, and take a cab ride from an Algerian up to Avignon. He gets paid in cash. I utilize one of my old drop houses and pick up a much smaller bundle of cash and three different IDs. Next to the Palais des Papes, I find a hotel at the end of an alley with no internet service and no links to any crew I know of. It's the perfect spot to wait and see. I told Nordeen I didn't want to track mess in his house with this. In truth, I don't want to bring him anywhere near Yasmine.

"You're a king playing the role of vizier to sycophants and insignificants" were the first words the boss said to me. They were coughed out between battles against rising sputum, sometimes settling in a draw. Behind me Fou-Fou, Suleiman, and a host of other loyal murderers sat outside the door. I felt most of their pulses rise, their throats close, and their jaws clench as we set about entering the room and approached the small sand igloo that the man rested in. As usual he was covered in blankets and shadows. I made out two eyes perched immediately over a pit of darkness, all a child's height above the ground. But nothing else.

I'd never met anyone I couldn't feel before. Still haven't, though I'm sure there are others out there. At the time, it was the first confirmed surprise regarding my power I'd experienced. Nordeen had no heartbeat, pulse, respiratory functions, or even digestive system that I could feel. Every time those deep yellow orbs that he calls eyes blinked, I was surprised. That was probably why it took me a few minutes to respond to his critique of my life.

"Why king?" I finally attempted in English, realizing I couldn't recall what language he had spoken to me in. "Why not God?"

"At best you might become a proper tuner of a god machine, little healer." He responded in English, after a laugh that frightened me more than I thought possible. "But your providence is what—bodies? Flesh? Perhaps time even? The gods are beyond such things."

"I'm barely understanding what you're saying. Are you like me?"

"You are barely visible as one of my kin, little healer. Don't presume too much." There was spittle in his voice that brightened the room as he spoke. It came to me that the others stayed out of the room not out of deference to me but to him. "That the fates make your talent so capricious is your only value."

"You know what I can do?"

"Do you know? I asked you earlier. Do you work all flesh, animal, fish, and fowl? Is your trick limited to the body, or do you see the mind and spirit as well? How do you heal? Do you reverse the ravages of time? Or do you connect to the eternal ideal of the flesh and return it to that monstrously stagnant vision? Speak quickly and know I cannot be lied to." It was the only hint he ever gave me of his own abilities. I told him everything that I knew about my powers, though I left out my brother and my time in London with Yasmine. As soon as he said it, I believed he could tell if I was lying. I banked on omissions not being considered lies. But there was enough in my initial diatribe to make my soon-to-be master/boss content.

"From the sounds of it, you are a true healer. Unedited in the corporal connections amongst humans. You will serve my purpose well, if you so desire." He coughed hard, and in those spasms I saw severely taxed organs illuminate from under his blankets. Whether it was with my power or with the naked eye, I can't tell to this day. He seemed to be a man unimpressed with shocking others, so I did my best to conceal my surprise.

"You mean I have a choice?"

"Life worker." He attempted a smile. "You above all others should know that when there is life, there is always choice. I will not hold you here. Tomorrow my men and I will be gone. If you decide to come with us, I will teach you as much as I can about the thing that has decided to rest inside of you. My payment will be your undying loyalty for as long as I deem fit. You will be taken care of. You will have to work, but it won't be hard for you. In time, you will come to appreciate it."

"I've worked for warlords before . . ."

"Yes, in Mogadishu. That was where you first came to my attention. And as you walked across the original lands to the first tribes who speak to the stars, you carved an arc of healing . . . heralding your presence to all who would look for those such as us."

"So why not kings then?" I asked trying to have a conversation instead of an interview. "Why not let whoever wants to find me, find me. If they are gods, I'll bow. But if they're men, let them come for me. I'll just heal myself."

"I remember when I was your age and just as ignorant, little healer. Yet I pride myself on learning lessons from the past. So I shall not, as my teacher did, bury you in a well with a one-ton rock resting on it to test how long it takes you to build up your strength to climb and lift the rock. Suffice to say, there are fates worse than death that those such as we can inflict on one as limited as yourself." I shook at the idea.

"You didn't want the others in here." My head was beginning to hurt from the massive amounts of information Nordeen gave with every sentence.

"They are not like us. Tell any of them what I am, and I promise you a slow death." I started in shock, truly afraid for the first time in ages that I would be murdered. "The prologue to your necessary knowledge, little healer is this: the more people who know what you are, the more people are likely to use it against you." I backed out of the room at that point, making a point to keep my gaze below the two yellow globes.

If you can understand why I stayed with Nordeen, then you can understand me a little better. I'm not a sycophant. I don't crave power, nor do I have a desire to be under anyone who does. Nordeen's description of the power inside of me was perfect: "the thing that decided to take up residence inside of me." On rough days, it made me feel like an alien beast or, as Yasmine would say, like a freak. But on good days, when I exercised my power in right relation to the world, I felt nearly unstoppable. I grew with power.

Living a bipolar life, rocketing between freak and human, made me long for some stability. And despite the bowel-spilling terror Nordeen invoked, he offered that. I knew that under his protection and guidance I would learn more about myself.

If you don't have powers, then you probably can't understand why I stayed. Best analogy I can come up with is this: imagine you're a gorilla living amongst chimps. Yeah, they're kind of like you, but they're lighter, smaller, less substantial. They run around afraid all the time, screaming and barking at the slightest sound. You can throw your weight around and get whatever you want. So when you finally come across another gorilla, not only another gorilla, but an older, stronger gorilla that has a crew of chimps doing his bidding without doing much weight throwing, you want to figure out how it all goes down.

Still, I knew Nordeen was serious about his loyalty pledge. I'd seen the razors around Fou-Fou's neck. And I spent half a sleepless night imaging what depraved things Nordeen would have me doing, and what would happen if I tried to run. I was afraid to even think too loudly for fear of him hearing my thoughts. But I spent the rest of the night imaging the worlds and possibilities the shadow man could show me. After my brother and Yasmine, I'd only met one other person like me: the boy from the Mog. The way Nordeen spoke, it was as though he knew all of the people like us in the world. I had learned more about my power from the Mog boy than from all my anatomy classes, and the kid was barely ten. So I couldn't afford to put distance between me and Nordeen.

I met him again in his cobbled-together cave the next day. Again, my gaze was low, but this time I crawled in excited. I told him I wanted to leave with them. I expected some form of welcome.

"Come and heal me then. Learn what you can from that, and let it be the seal on your healing for a year." My family was never the religious type. I'd been to church maybe ten times in my life. But when I reached out to lay hands on this man whose full body I still couldn't totally perceive, it felt like I was about to touch a holy icon. Touching his skin, an organ I'm used to feeling in my body long before I connect to it with my hand, was bracing. It held me tight, like a quick-growing fungus with deadly intent. At the same time my senses, and my special sense, were being flooded by an . . . intoxicating invisible liquid. I found myself ravenous and full at the same time, freezing and flush, dangerously open and totally intimate. In the end, it was up to him to break our contact. In a flash of insight I saw disappointment in what Nordeen perceived as his own weakness. I couldn't help but remember what the Dogon had said about healers being the death of the warrior's spirit.

A day and a half in Avignon touring the streets, and I can't figure out if I'm just too bat-shit to realize no one's actually following me, or if I'm just too anxious to truly notice. I've still got another day paid up at the hotel, but I make my way to the train anyway and take the first one to Paris. I open my head on the train and take in all the bodies on the way with me. In my car alone three people have genetic diseases—ALS, sickle-cell, and the beginnings of Tay-Sachs—things I'd have to focus on all day to do anything with. Even then I could only do one a month. Five people have myelin-sheathing issues, either too much or too little. A seven-year-old boy will become blind because of it next week. A five-year-old girl has some sort of chronic respiratory distress. Her blood's not fully oxygenated and hasn't been for a while. Neglectful parents, or someone's too busy cheating on their wife to notice; chronic respiratory problem girl's dad has gonorrhea, her mom doesn't.

The woman with the smell of donkey sausage on her hands behind me has broken two bones in her life. Ten people have hypertension. Five people are drunk. I'm swimming in their biorhythms.

"Ticket, please," the conductor asks me. Missed him. Damn. I just felt a mass of cells and neurons. I give him his billet, and he stops looking at me as a hobo. At least temporarily. Fuck him. Parkinson's is maybe five years away for that guy.

I'm not mad at him, really. More at myself. I'm used to combat situations where I can trash about recklessly or covert ops where no one knows what I can do and I operate with impunity. To do this right I have to blend in. I have to have total access to my skills and not look like an epileptic who forgot his medication as I utilize them. Chewing gum and walking. It shouldn't be hard, but it's the price I'm paying for living in virtual solitude for the past few years.

I can't remember the last time I was in Paris. Razor-neck tends to stay away from tourist traps. We've got people in Clichy-sous-Bois, some suburbs in the east, but they've only been there three months. Still, I could call them, I think. Then . . . FUCK! I'm solo in this. No razor-neck. I'm grabbing the razor around my neck, letting it cut into my hand. I want to yank it off and send it sailing. But something primitive and scared deep in my belly in a place even my powers can't see demands I don't. I've seen enough of it to know the razor is indstructible. I'm afraid of what other dark tricks it might possess. Instead I find a pay phone.

I dial numbers I thought I'd forgotten. It works just like the former CIA spook I paid to set it up said it would. I wait for a clean minute then hear a tone like a fax machine trying to dial in. I punch in another set of numbers, my brother's ID number on his psych-ward bracelet, and I retrieve messages. No amicable operator telling me what numbers to press. One to hear, two to advance, three to erase.

Yasmine's voice sends my heart into spasms again. Cayenne-flavored honey. Extended vowels to cover a slight lisp. Well-manicured teeth massaged by a tongue that's mastered so many languages she gets them confused in casual conversations. I know she's hurt. I know it's not fake. I know she called me a freak. I don't care. I'm coming. I punch two sixes and a nine. No way Suleiman could know about it. It's an automatic phone trace. You'd have to be another client of the CIA spook to get around it. The number spits back in robot Farsi and I memorize it. Then it's two nines and a six. The line is dead and buried in the ground so deep down the devil couldn't find it in hell. It was worth the ten grand to set up. I hang up the phone and pickpocket a cell phone from a café. I quick-dial the number. I hear a British "Hello?" I ask for Yasmine. They don't know who I'm talking about. I ask who I'm talking to. A bloke on a street phone is what he says. Can't be more than seventeen years old. His voice just cracked. What city I ask. "London, yaw tosser." He hangs up. I wonder if she's moved from the apartment.

The last time I saw Yasmine was seven years ago. I had been work-ing for Nordeen for a year and a half, mostly watching and using my passport as a shield for the young men who were becoming less afraid of me and more like friends. Suleiman was the number two. Everyone knew it. I was the voice box. I held Nordeen's opinions but had no final say on actions. When drama jumped off in Rome, in Segovia, in Prague, I stood up and fired back just like the rest of the crew, more afraid of the boss than the bullets passing overhead. I'd been around guns for a while, and while no expert, I knew how to shoot and run at the same time. That was a passable enough skill amongst the razor-necks. But it was also evident the boss and I had a special connection.

Not using my powers was disconcerting. At first it was like being sighted but refusing to see. I felt retarded, simple, delayed. I asked Nordeen why he'd made me promise.

"You and the thing inside of you must figure out who is the boss. Just because it keeps you alive does not mean you are in control. Think back to your trek across the original lands. Your skin darker, better to absorb the sun, your feet more calloused to protect from burs and thorns. Your scent even changed, causing confusion amongst the beasts. But which of these changes did you dictate? When you heal, are you conscious of what you are doing or is it more instinct?"

"Instinct," I said quickly. "All the more reason to develop skill, yes?"

"I agree." He smiled that ruthless smile again. "I didn't say not to use your power."

It was true. He had only told me no more healing. Took me about a month and another bullshit crossfire over bullshit, not even work, in Manchester with a bunch of Australians for me to get it. Two razors hit on the wrong women in the wrong bar and the wrong Aussies caught wind of it. Bar fight. On instinct my bones went denser as my muscles snaked stealthily around them, enabling me to catch a brawler's fist in my open hand. The boss's prohibition still rang in my mind, along with our recent conversation. I held the Aussie's arm tight, and for the first time I thought about what else I could do to a flesh and bone aside from healing. In a second I dissolved every tendon in his arm by redirecting his stomach acids. The Aussie fell like a brick. I felt like I'd spit on a cross or pissed on a Koran. Imagine thinking in reverse, or breathing backward. I made a body do what it shouldn't. The Aussie's scream alone broke up the rest of the fight. I felt his vocal cords straining as he made a sound that should never come from a human throat. I did it with a touch. And so I ran.

Bar fight be damned. I'd realized my potential for destruction to the human body. I did it on instinct, the same way I healed. I was a freak, and so I went to the only woman who had ever properly named me. I took the van we'd all driven up in and sprinted down to London where I hoped she still lived. In the three-hour drive, I had time to actually think about what I'd done. It was the first time I'd used my power to hurt. Even when I beat my brother, I did it with my fists alone. But with this new development, I felt closer to him than I ever had before. Closer to him, and to Nordeen. His twisted smile beamed out from an inky blackness in my mind. He knew this would happen. He saw the pain and discomfort not using my powers caused. His little suggestions were enough to get me thinking in the wrong direction. I'd fulfilled his bent desires and prophecies, and now my spirit was twisted, too.

Of course, I'd also just run from the man while still wearing his razor around my neck. I couldn't care. I was too distraught from the pain I had previously thought the province of my brother. I scurried back to my only family, to my lost love.

The apartment, in an up-and-coming section of Brixton, was where we'd first settled. It was still occupied, but my years away had seen the neighborhood change; like Yasmine, it had become classier than its roots. I felt beyond out of place, but it didn't matter. The second-story flat overlooking the old skate park was still lit. Dusk had turned to night hours ago, but I could still make out her outline in silhouette at the window. I relaxed in the van, parking across the street, and reached out with my senses just to "feel" her body. I expected comfort. I should've known better.

Her body had changed. She had had a tumor. A seven-pound eight-ounce tumor that she held inside of her for nine months before releasing it into the world. She'd given birth. It read like an old wound on her womb, her hips, her breasts. But they'd all long since healed. Her child was at least six years old, by the feel of it. I choked, cutting my probe off so suddenly she was bound to notice. When we were together she had become accustomed to my searching her body for any signs of infection or disease. It's a type of intimacy one has a hard time forgetting. Yasmine came to the window quickly, searching the streets. I sunk lower into my seat, realizing I was doing the exact opposite of what I'd set out from Manchester to do. I didn't have long to sink. A limousine pulled up to our old apartment, hers now, and a black-suited man in a gray tie exited. Maybe seven years her, our, senior, his pale skin, rakish frame, and blemished skin told me he was British. He bounded up the stairs to the front gate. My stomach turned with the possibility I knew would prove fact. In no time, Yasmine descended, a small girl in tow, looking more refined and polished than I'd ever given her opportunity to be. The girl had her mother's hair, her smile, and the rake's bounce in her step.

She hadn't waited for me. There were no reasonable grounds to think she would've. Didn't stop me from thinking it, though. Didn't stop me from crying in the van, calling myself a freak for over an hour. When I was done, I called the only one who understood me.

"To be king, you would have to be as them. You can never be like them" was all Nordeen said when I called. No "Hello," not even an acknowledgment of who I was. When I asked if there was any way I could come back, he laughed. "Why do you think you left? I have business in London. Put yourself some place nice and wait for instructions," he said with the kindness of a grandfather. It was the first hint of genuine affection I'd ever felt from him. I was smart enough not to bank on it again. A few days later the rest of the crew would come down. No questions asked about my disappearance or the pain I'd caused in the Aussie. In fact, no mention of the bar fight at all. The only evidence I had of anything having occurred at all was the returned reluctance of Fou-Fou and Suleiman to touch me. The others didn't share the reservation, but I got the sense it was because they actually didn't remember what happened.

In turn, I told them nothing about Yasmine. I did my boss's bidding along with the rest of the crew. There was a mid-level street gang gaining more power every day in Hackney. Nordeen wanted to know what they were about, if they were to be made allies or tombstones. We tested their mettle through emissaries, hiring other local crews to take shots at them, and found that either our intermediaries weren't up to the task or the Hackney boys had come by their reps honestly. In the end Nordeen ordered us to deliver a small Ethiopian woman, maybe eighteen years old, to their big man, a black giant of a proper East Ender who never looked excited but whose heartbeat constantly raced. He accepted the woman like he knew who she was. She never said a word, and none of us were dumb enough to ask about it. I was tempted to "feel" more of his body or hers, but my powers had shown me enough new tricks for a while.

The whole bizarre fiasco lasted three months. It, more than anything, made me wonder about Nordeen Maximus. He'd sent his Number 2 and his healer off to foreign lands and didn't seem pressed about it. He even gave us fifteen thousand dollars each when we were done and told us to take a week off before making our own ways back to Morocco.

I used ten thousand dollars of that money to set up the phone. Then I wrote a note giving Yasmine the number, telling her not to leave her name or how to find her on the message but to call if she ever needed help.

It's true that I was a freak, and in her own quiet way, so was Yasmine, but I'd done enough ear hustling around Nordeen to realize there were bigger freaks with real sadistic tendencies out there. Nordeen told me about a person like us who killed others like us just to prove it could be done. I didn't want Yasmine stumbling into one of those freaks and not having anyone to call on. I've never stopped loving her. I can't.

Chapter Six

It was less the cold than the predominance of pale faces that surprised me as I came into Heathrow. The London of my memory was so multiethnic it felt almost forced at times. But the airport was populated with a majority of white travelers and colored staff. It only distracted me for a second. Then it was back to work.

I'm thinking about the best way to search out Yasmine. I've still got some contacts over here. It wouldn't be too hard for them to run a trace. But if they know where she is, then they can sell that information—or have it beaten, burned, or shot out of them. Until I know what's going on, I've got to do this solo. I'm about to get on the tube and hit the old apartment, hoping she's still there, when I see she hasn't been there for a while. I pick up a paper from the stand and see her face plastered all over the cover. "Diplomat's Daughter Still Missing," reads the headline. "Family Distraught."

I'm on the train heading to Piccadilly Square. Destination's not important, just need the time it takes to read the paper. She's been gone for a month now. Scotland Yard and MI5 are clueless. They're still not sure if it's a kidnapping or a runaway case, but all attempts to contact the fourteen-year-old, to ask her to just call and let her family know she's okay, have yielded nothing. Pictures of her are up everywhere, and the BBC has her picture on TV every hour on the hour.

The story has everyone talking because of the timing. Yasmine's husband is the diplomat. Of course he is. He's considered the go-to man for appropriate humanitarian-aid advice. I guess some people haven't been too happy with the aid he's offering, while others are miffed at not getting enough. No one's claiming responsibility for the kidnapping, but as the weeks drag on, it's seeming more and more of a possibility. Parliament, in its ultimate wisdom, is debating whether to suspend all humanitarian aid to foreign countries until this crisis is properly contained. While Mr. Shining Knight diplomat is thoroughly against the proposal, his raging against Parliament in this arena is what's keeping the story in the news.

This situation is filled with everything I do not want. Number one, the spotlight. With MI5 and Scotland Yard on it, if I make any kind of move on Yasmine, I'm getting flagged. While I don't have an official record anywhere, I'm one of the more suspicious characters who could be associating with a diplomat's wife. Number two, she went a married a damn diplomat, which could be code for MI5 handler or just a civic-minded nitwit who doesn't realize how little humanitarian aid can actually do. Number three, everyone, and I mean everyone, knows about this. Any chance of using my undercover skills and contacts went out the window a month ago, when newspapers and TV started blaring about the situation. Truth of it is, I'm the wrong guy for this. Either the girl ran away or she's been kidnapped. If she ran away, I'm too far removed from the London scene to be much help. If she was kidnapped, I would've been able to help if they hadn't been showing her face everywhere, making any reasonable person in the kidnapping profession completely wary of any new operators in their vicinity. I'm off the train before I know it, about to go back to Heathrow.

I'm waiting on the opposite platform when I notice someone reading the same paper as me. On the front page I see her again, Yasmine. She's holding tight to her man's jacket as they try and get through a sea of cameras. It's that face she only she puts on when all the others are unavailable. She is defeated. It looks like she's stalwart and tough. But I know her better. She's got nothing. The diplomat is waving his arms around high above her head, trying to get the paparazzi to leave them alone. Yasmine cowers under him, but she isn't that much shorter than him. Her knees are buckling. God, she's beautiful.

Fine. Maybe I can't help her. But I can try. I'm special. I can do things. I know people.

I'm seeing things in this photo that no one else could. She's grieving. But the picture, her huddled below her man, is a sham. Her eyes don't turn that way, and her crow's feet aren't that close together. Someone doctored the photo. She didn't seem distraught enough. That's my woman. She doesn't get overwhelmed or sad—she gets angry. The truth of the picture is in her hands. She's grasping her man's jacket tight, not for support, but to have something to grip rather than a photographer's neck. The veins are tight, lots of blood coursing through them. She's been working out.

I get off the train near Piccadilly Square and search for an internet café. It takes all of a minute. I buy two hours of time and some disaster of a caffeinated beverage along with a too-sweet tart. I'll have to get used to Western food again.

I don't start with her. She's always been private, not wanting anyone to know even the first thing about her. It's why she was a reporter: so she could tell other people's stories. She never even wanted our number listed. If people knew too much, they might connect her to the rash of fires she started as a child, before she got her power under control. They might find out she was a freak. She only showed me what she could do with fire by accident. I molested a roasted-chicken dinner, which led to the kitchen curtains going up in flames. She talked the flames down, then passed out. I took care of her until she woke up, realizing the whole time that I'd never be able to stop loving her. We exchanged stories that night. About who we were and how we wanted to be seen. . . .

✳

But she made a detour on the mystery path. She married a camera hog. He doesn't come off as it, but it takes a lot to be in the news at least once a month for five years. Darren Bridgecombe comes from fish-and-chips, literally. His parents owned a fish-and-chip shop in Derry, before it became a curry joint in the eighties. At sixteen he did his first volunteering overseas in Jordan, teaching Arabs how to speak like Brits. An interview he gave four years ago says he became "obsessed with making education available for the world on that trip." Self-righteous prick. Same interview says his next major trip abroad was to Sri Lanka. He beat me there by a good eight years. He says that interviewing both sides in that scrap was what led him to his theory of world peace through equitable distribution of knowledge. Guess you've got to be like Fish'n'Chips and have a master's in economics and education to understand that one. I sure as hell don't.

Right out of university, the permanent Under-Secretary for Foreign Affairs scoops him as a speechwriter. I read three of the speeches then take a bite out of the oversweet pastry. I wonder which one has more filling?

About fourteen years ago, the undersecretary changes Fish'n'Chips's job description to unofficial ambassador of education. He goes to Liberia, where he meets Yasmine. Some gossip rag that tries to pass itself off as legitimate news by only gossiping about politicians asks him how long the courting process was. He says it was love at first sight. I almost retch.

The press knows Yasmine as notoriously shy. She never gave an interview before her girl was kidnapped. Even then her words are sparse. Never any back-and-forth interviews, only statements. They've all got this undercurrent of anger in them.

I'm image-searching for them when I get what I need. It's from last year. A photo taken near the family home as the three of them head out for a walk. The girl's taken Yasmine's naturally red hair and gone a step brighter. Tamara, they call the girl, keeps her hair long, down to her waist. She's a camera hog, looking almost inappropriately at the lenses trained on her father. Yasmine has a put-on smile, while authentically trying to hide from the flashbulbs behind her husband. She doesn't play the ethnically ambiguous wife of the up-and-coming politician very well. The thirteen-year-old is in front of him; hand on her hip, leaning forward in a pose she's seen in a thousand music videos. She's more focused on the humor of the situation than anything else.

The picture's irrelevant. It's the caption "The Bridgecombe family takes a well-deserved stroll around their new neighborhood in Kennington." She lives in Kennington now. Shouldn't be too hard to find her.

Two hours before the sun comes up the next morning, a hotel staff member's ulcer pain wakes me up. She knocks on my door. The ache on her ankles tells me she's been on her feet more than twelve hours. I don't open the door. I know she'll be back. Probably Nigerian, maybe from a poorer Kenyan family. Back when I was living here, the posh hotels only had white help. But more than ever London's an international city now, full of ethnic underclasses from every landmass in the world. So many of the poor and unwashed need jobs that even the Charos Grand Hotel, with its excellent view of the most gaudy tourist attraction on the planet, the London Eye, hires them. Creature comforts and the rest be damned, I chose the hotel for its centrality and its order-in-anything service. The concierge looked cross-eyed at me when I paid a week in advance with cash, but the extra tip got me the type of suite I wanted: on the least populated floor and far away from that damn Ferris wheel. The suite is impressive; Suleiman and his family could all fit in here comfortably. A bedroom, a main chamber, a kitchenette of sorts, and a full-sized bathtub. Plus there's a glass wall facing the office building across the street. Early morning light bounces off of those windows and reflects into my eyes if I don't close the blinds. Other than that the room is perfect. Too perfect for a black guy who pays in cash, I remind myself.

The boss got me to figure out how to change the way I look. How to change my bone structure, my body fat, my fingerprints, even my teeth. It was one of few times I saw joy in his dehydrated face. "Now you are truly useful," he told me.

I make myself two shades lighter and force my hair to grow about five inches longer. I compact my vertebrae and shrink my thigh and arm bones so that I am effectively about three inches shorter. I smooth out the forehead and cheek wrinkles that desert and beach living have graced me with. In the mirror I smile at my lie. I look like I'm twenty-one again.

I meet London early morning after a big breakfast of ham, steak, egg and cheese, biscuits, potatoes, toast, coffee, and tea. I'm not hungry. It's all ammunition. I don't know what this day will bring, but if it's lots of metabolic changes in me or lots of healing for someone else, I'll need energy. I'm in the neighborhood of the fish'n'chips boy before the first commuters wake. I'm wearing a black and red Adidas running suit I picked up yesterday, across the street from the internet café. As I walk I'm stretching my legs like I'm about to go for a major run. Like I need to. My hood is down. I want everyone watching Yasmine to be watching me, seeing this face. I give them five minutes of the bullshit stretches people who run all the time have to do. Normal people. I'm feeling for Yasmine. Her biorhythms are so familiar to me, even now it's painful. I don't mean to wake her up, but I flutter her. Then I take off.

The phone book listed five gyms in the general area of their flat. One is way too grimy to be of use to Yasmine. My run reveals another as being too popular. Who goes to the gym at six in the morning? I narrow it down to three, and pick the one easiest to get to. I throw my senses wide for the woman I love while I ask for a day pass, and as I sit through a pushy offer to join the gym, I luck out. She's here. There's a pud in front of me I wouldn't waste time to smack, babbling away as though he and I were the best of friends while the woman I *should* be spending the rest of my life with is walking right by me. And she doesn't even recognize me.

The years have been more than kind to her. Even the last time I saw her, through the window of our old place, in that black silk dress that looked too good for me to put my hands on, even then she didn't look as good as she does now. It was like her beauty was waiting until her body grew to an appropriate age to fully manifest. She doesn't wear a lick of makeup, not even some base-color lipstick. She's got hips, and enough of a rounded ass to not be confused with a flat-butted Brit chick. Her hair, short-cropped and showing the first signs of gray, is pulled back in a tight bun resting just above the base of her neck. By the time she exits the changing room and climbs on the elliptical machine, she's sporting a dark green top that holds her small breasts close, and black tights that hold that beautiful ass even closer. I'm visibly distracted. The idiot ranter is finally giving up the ghost and giving me a trial day pass as an endurance prize for putting up with his bullshit. Despite temptation, I do a once-around the gym, targeting anyone that came in after her. Each one could be MI5.

After a sip of water I'm giving the sixty-five-year-old with carpal tunnel trying to jazzercise his way backward from his next heart attack a dopamine rush he hasn't felt since he lost his virginity, sometime around when the first *Dr. Who* came on. He's stunned—any more of his runner's high will leave him with stains on his pants. I slide next to Yasmine, who notices nothing with her headphones on.

I want to apologize for all the things I've thought. I want to get down on my knees and beg her to forget about Fish'n'Chips and her missing kid. I want to sell her identity to Nordeen, so she'll be in the same ambiguous bind as I am. I want her on top of me screaming in my ear to not stop. I want her to never know how to write the word "freak." My pulse is a speed-metal techno beat. My heart thinks my chest cavity is just a mirage. I've forgotten how to swallow. I've forgotten which glands will give me saliva. I'm about to speak when she looks at me. We both stop the elliptical machines. There was a better way to do this, other than looking like my twenty-one-year-old self again. But I don't know how.

"I'm sorry." Her voice is the same cayenne-flavored honey. Randomly accented thanks to parents who couldn't figure out what continent to settle on. "You look like someone I used to know."

"It's me," is all I can get out.

"Taggert?"

"You called. I came." There's no lie in it.

Chapter Seven

"You look . . ."

"Yeah, I kn—"

"You look the same, Tag."

"Nobody calls me Tag anymore."

"But you look the same!"

"Keep it down."

"Why?"

"MI5, Scotland Yard, whoever the hell is looking in your direction."

"No one is looking at me. I'm a low-level politician's wife whose daughter ran away."

"Ran away? I thought—"

"You look the same!"

"It's part of what I can do. Put it together, Mene! I heal hurts right? What's aging but protracted hurt done by living?"

Silence. Then she talks.

"Why like that?"

"Like what? This is me."

"That's you from fourteen years ago. Have you not changed since . . . ?"

"I've changed more than you know."

Silence again. This time she steps off the elliptical machine before she speaks.

"We should go somewhere."

"I'll wait outside."

I don't smoke. I drink, because most people I'm around do and it puts them at ease. It takes more effort for me to feel the effects of alcohol than it's worth, but I put up with it. Point is, I've got no vices. They're important. They give you something to do other than stand around and look nervous while the only woman you've ever loved changes into her street clothes inside a gym.

It's full morning now. Respectable morning. Seven-thirty in the morning. The streets are bustling. I grab two coffees from a Turkish street vendor. Yasmine exits the gym looking like the most efficient heartbreaker on the planet. Where semi-skintight gear used to hug her, she's sporting a button-up white silk blouse with blue stripes, and a pumpkin-colored skirt that lies to your eyes when they ask where the cloth ends and the ass begins. Still no makeup. Still no bullshit. As I hand her the coffee, she's got her professional voice on.

"I need to know why you're here." Dry as a Bedouin's tongue.

"You called. I came." The repetition of my answer startles her.

"This . . . this isn't about you and me?"

"This is about your daughter."

"For me." She nods, searching my face for comprehension. "But what is this for you?"

"This is me coming because you asked. You want me gone, say go. I'll leave knowing my word is still good. But it sounds like you need some help. You want it, I'm here. You don't . . ."

"Tamara didn't run away."

"Speak on it." I follow her lead on the mad dash through crowds that seem to part the way for the both of us. Four inches shorter than I am now and she still makes way through the crowd like a linebacker.

"It's more convenient for everyone to think that she's just some brat who wanted more attention and decided taking off for a few weeks was the perfect way to get it. She wouldn't do that. I know her." This is all she'll say until we reach a café by the Thames. I sit down silent, like a good dog, and wait. The waiter gives us menus, but she doesn't even bother with the pretense of opening hers before ordering pastries and coffee for the both of us.

"I never lied to Tamara. Never gave her any reason to lie to me. She was a typical teenager, yes. She smoked hash about every other weekend. I wasn't proud of it, but I didn't malign her because of it. She had a boyfriend last year, but he broke up with her because she wouldn't shag him. That wasn't my direction but her own. You understand, Tag? She has her own principles. . . ."

"Did you tell her about me?" She's about to answer when the bloody waiter comes back. She takes spins around the coffee rim with her spoon, then answers in a deliberate voice that lets me know I've crossed the line.

"I told her that I was in love with someone else once. Before her father. But that our lifestyles didn't coincide."

"Makes me sound like a dope fiend."

"Better a dope fiend than a—"

"Don't say freak!" I'm too loud. It's a novice mistake of mine, to shape my vocal cords temporarily for greater volume. Maybe the cooks in the back didn't hear, but everyone else does. I shake my head slowly, preparing to apologize.

"I . . . I wasn't going to use that word," she says.

"Stay away from euphemisms as well, if you don't mind."

"I . . . can't apologize for that, Tag. I was younger then, harsher. I didn't mean to . . ." She's expecting me to stop her. I don't even try. "Was it a mistake to call you?"

"Depends on why you did in the first place."

"My daughter didn't run away. Someone chased her away, or she's staying away for a reason. No one else will find her. They think its part of a political ploy ever since Darren took a stand against the sympathy vote in Parliament."

"Darren." I didn't realize I'd said it until it came out of my mouth.

"Hey!" She barks at me like I'd just trashed the man's name. "He is my husband. He is Tamara's father. And he's a good man."

"If he's such a good man, then why isn't he trying to find his daughter right now instead of making speeches to this permanent undersecretary and that budget director? And what the fuck is a permanent undersecretary anyway? And since when did you find politicians so goddamn sexy?" She's so smart it's scary. She just sits back and waits until I condense it all down to one question. "Did you cheat on me with him?"

"By the time I left for Liberia, it was done, Taggert. I was done. You had . . ." She's calling the waiter over for more coffee. She hasn't even taken a bite out of her pastry. I check the activity of the acid in her stomach and find its hasn't broken down anything in over thirty hours. But it's getting more agitated with every passing second. My fault.

"Tell me what you know about Tamara disappearing."

"No," she says softly. "This could all be a mistake, Taggert. I was . . . I am desperate. I'm grasping at straws. You're a straw. That's it. I'd be a total liar if I said I didn't think about you all these years. But that was my adolescence. I look back on it fondly, but I don't miss it. I don't miss you. I miss . . ." I feel her tear ducts giving before she does. I'm telling myself it's sympathy pains that cause mine to go when hers do. "I miss my baby. I miss my little girl. I want my little girl. I'll do whatever I have to do to find her. No one else cares, Tag. Everybody thinks she ran away, but she wouldn't do that to me. Do you see what I'm saying? She just wouldn't do that to me."

She wipes her face with her sleeve, takes a small napkin and blows her nose briefly but fiercely. The red puffiness about her eyes and cheeks won't go away for another couple of minutes, but her voice returns to its solid calm in a matter of seconds.

"I called you because I think you can help find my daughter. I didn't call you because I love you or I miss you or I need you or anything like that. If that's your hope, and I contributed to that in any way, then I'm sorry . . . and let's say good-bye now. I love my family. I love my daughter and I love my husband." I'm taking the blows like a champ even though each one feels like a wooden stake through my vampiric heart. I feel like an ass for wanting her, pining away for over a decade. I'm feeling like even more of an ass for wanting to run away from the situation. "Prove that you were right." The thing that lives inside me whispers every time I attempt to leave. It's the only thing keeping me stuck to my seat.

I chose my powers. I chose my life, the grime and grit of it. I chose to go where people hurt the most, in order to find the best ways to heal. It was in that choosing that I found Nordeen, and he's shown me the shadows of the real rulers of the planet. Not politicians and businessmen but gods and powers most people don't have the concepts, let alone the names, to explain. I can't remember when I stopped thinking about money as evidence of my self-worth, but it was long before I met the boss. I've been removed from the common psychology of men for longer than I can recall. I may be a freak, but unlike you, Yasmine, I embraced my freakiness. And in doing so, in knowing what it meant to be a freak, I've turned myself into an invaluable resource to men and demigods alike. You chose a man who hopes to do once what I perform regularly. You rejected your fire only to now call on mine. And I came. Not because it's the right thing to do. But to prove you wrong. To show you the value of a freak. To prove to you I was right.

But this is only what I think. I couldn't ever say such things to her.

"I'm not a private investigator," I say slowly so she'll understand it's not an attack.

"But you cut a healing swathe through some of the most diseased and forlorn parts of Africa."

47

"You heard about that?"

"I'm an international reporter of human-rights cases, Tag. How is some random man walking through Africa ignoring tribal, political, and territorial lines healing the sick not going to come across my radar? People hailed you as a messiah." She pauses, and I know she's got more. "Did you know you cured one woman of AIDS?"

"Yes." She's not Nordeen, so I enjoy my ability to lie. I didn't know. It doesn't matter. There's awe in her voice. Eat your heart out, Fish'n'Chips.

"It's the only documented case of faith healing of HIV on the books. There's a two-million-euro live bounty out for your head based on her description alone. . . ."

"What does this have to do with your daughter?"

"She's . . ." Her voice is lower than it's ever been. Not just since the gym, but since I've known her. I don't know if she's talking to herself or to me. "She's like you."

"She's a healer?" Why am I so excited?

"No. She can move things . . . with her mind."

"Telekinetic?"

"Yes. But she also can hear thoughts . . . telepathic. That's what it is." I'm angry and don't bother hiding it.

"What?" she barks at me from too far of an emotional distance to expect to be heard. "What did I say? What did I do?"

"Call on a freak to catch a freak?" She slaps me hard enough to break one of her fingers. Other customers react. I don't.

"My daughter is not a freak!"

"But I am?" She has no words for me. Instead she drops a twenty-pound note on the table and walks out the door. I take a second to survey the restaurant, to see if anyone follows her. When no one else does, I do. She's at a railing overlooking the Thames. After a minute, I join her.

"This was a mistake," she says, holding her hands tight below her chin, praying.

"No. You made the right call. Just to the wrong man. Bigger man, better man, would be able to put the past aside for the sake of an innocent and all that valiant shit. Me? I'm still more like this face than I'd care to admit. A child playing grown-up games."

"I need you to be that man now," she says softly like we've never passed a harsh word between us. "You're the only one I know like her. . . ."

"Like you." I'm reminding her.

"Like me," she concedes begrudgingly. "Tamara had just come to her . . . skills, power, whatever you call it. She told me about it."

"Did you tell her about me and—"

"I told her that I had something similar." She truly loved her daughter. Once we moved to London, Yasmine stopped experimenting with her fire totally. Not even to light a candle. Whenever I pushed her on it, we had fights that would wake neighbors. I asked her one time what it felt like to start fires. I wanted to know if it was in the realm of possibilities for me to cauterize a wound instead of making the blood vessels just atrophy. She said starting fires was like dropping acid into her worldview. Now I would see that as a sign of problems to come, but then I was too inexperienced in love, too needy to see it as an indication of anything other than my need to compromise more. "It made her feel . . . better."

"Just because she's like us"—I wait to hear protestations against any type of union involving the two of us, and smile when they don't come—"that doesn't mean she'd be able to fight off whatever came her way. They could have drugged her. If she's not very experienced. . . ."

"That's not why I think it has to do with the . . ." She stops and looks at me. "Can I just see your face? This is so disconcerting. Can you show me what you look like now?" I relax into my own height, skin tone, weight, and facial features, all of it. It takes less than a minute. Any gawking commuters would get a shock, but they'd have to watch for that full minute. People in cities generally don't look at each other for over a few seconds.

The transition makes Yasmine sick. I can feel the bile rising in her throat. She wants to throw up. She just stares at me in fascination. "Thank you."

"It's just practice and precaution."

"I understand. Before she left, Tamara began acting secretive. . . ."

"You said the two of you were tight?"

"Not with me. With her father. She said things were going on. Things only I would understand, that might hurt him politically if she got involved. I didn't ask. She's getting older. I figured she had a right to a certain level of privacy. It's hard to always be in the public light. If I had known . . ."

"And so that's why you think it has to do with what we do?"

"What we can do, yes. She never displayed her . . . gifts. She was quiet about them. Once I had to chastise her for reading her teacher's mind during an exam. But she already felt so bad about it. In part because the things in a high school teacher's mind regarding his students are so depraved. . . ."

"I can't promise anything," I say, stretching my actual body, realizing the clothes I bought fit better on it.

"I'm not expecting promises. I don't think this is what you want, but I can give you—"

"I don't want your money, Yasmine." I'm trying not to sound hurt by the offer.

"What do you want?" The question takes me by surprise. "I've told you what I can't give you. You don't want what I can give. I know why I called you, Taggert. What I don't know is why you answered."

"Because I said I would."

I've met about twenty people like me. Three before I ran into Nordeen. My brother, Yasmine, and the kid from the Mog. Including Nordeen, that's sixteen or so I've met in the six years I've worked with the old man. Some of them have been old but young in their powers, others babies with the ability to dominate the world. Nordeen's approach to them is as enigmatic as it is decisive, and in most cases I am his messenger. So when Yasmine says she thinks this whole mess involves people like us, I gain more confidence than I've had since I left Morocco. If it's powers, I've probably got some experience with it.

When the boss figured out that I could hurt people, he began to use me as a smart gun. With a little practice I realized I didn't have to touch people to affect their bodies. All I needed was to be in range, to feel their heartbeats. My first kill using my power was in Agadir, a small costal city in Morocco. A supplier was threatening to break the distribution line. Nordeen sent me in first, to drink tea in the man's café. When he was assured I was there, Nordeen made the call. The dealer made the mistake of underestimating the boss. I squeezed his heart with my mind until it collapsed into a bloodied clump of muscle and vein. When I felt no remorse, I knew a line had been crossed. So did the boss when I returned.

"Now you are ready for the serious work."

"You're saying what I just did wasn't serious?"

"Killing one of them is as easy as swatting a fly. Taking out one of ours requires a steel of will and skill that I'm beginning to suspect you might have."

He sent me to India, just outside of Bangalore. He told me to find the most powerful one like us there, and to kill them. It turned out to be a six-year-old Jain boy who spoke to the dead and animated their bones for limited amounts of time. His power had made him insane, and his sole desire was to turn the entire town into a necropolis so he'd always have people in his mind to talk to.

"I can't do it," I told Nordeen over a cell phone.

"And why not? Is the death dealer too much for you?"

"He's six years old."

"Would you rather face him or me?"

I compromised and gave the kid an aneurysm. He couldn't speak, couldn't move, couldn't utilize his power, but he was still alive.

It was the same thing I did to my brother, but with far more subtlety. Nordeen greeted me upon my return with a reluctant welcome. He knew the boy wasn't dead but accepted my compromise despite the potential threat against his will. I was banished from his sight for three months.

He sent me throughout the world to meet other people like us. Sometimes he'd just have me identify the person. Other times he'd tell me to bring gifts, books that held the smell of antiquity, or fruits I couldn't identify. All the ones who I met and spoke with knew of Nordeen. Some spoke of him in hushed tones, others dismissed me and gave dire warnings for "my master." From dropped sentences and silenced thoughts, I got that I was not the first of Nordeen's emissaries. After a while I realized that the whole hash-dealing business was just a cover, a way of financing his true passion. Us.

After my exile, Nordeen took a trip with me. Johannesburg. An old woman whose skin looked like it was petrified and who kept roots and barks in multicolored glass jars suspended in the air had sent him an invitation in a dream. On the private plane ride down, I somehow felt that Nordeen had been injured and healed ... by someone else. I kept that knowledge to myself, as he seemed anxious for the first time in my experience.

The elder woman laughed when she saw me. "Old man, do you carry your healer with you everywhere these days?" Her voice broke the night sky above the tarmac, and small bits of fire jumped from her lips.

"I bring him as a courtesy to you, should I lose my temper and break off a part of you that even I can't fix," he replied with a honeyed voice. "Keep your sparks to yourself woman and guide me to our master." In an old cargo container, on an ancient rusting freighter, the two powers made ablutions for each other and walked into a darkness that no light would penetrate. Even the sparks from the old woman's tongue didn't emanate outward. I waited for twenty-four hours in a car on the dock wondering what power in the world existed that could cow my boss so. At the beginning of that second night, Nordeen emerged alone. He seemed revitalized physically, standing taller, his cane for ornamentation alone. His eyes shone brightly. And when he spoke, small sparks of fire came from his mouth.

"Never forget, little healer. There are powers stronger than ours in this world. And they do not always favor us."

Those words are on my mind as I think about how to hunt down this girl, this Tamara. The really powerful ones of our type attract others. Those others are so far above us they make us seem like the normals. If one of those others is involved in this, I'm screwed. But if not, I can do this.

The moderately powerful ones like us alienate our families. As my brother did. As I did. But the most powerful of us are always alone. So she can't be that powerful. Plus, she had to make a choice to read her teacher's mind. That means she either doesn't have the power to do it casually or she has that much control. Doesn't matter. Point is she's living a normal life. A normal life means normal boundaries, normal friends, normal schooling. And our kind of power among the norms always leaves trails.

I leave Yasmine and hit a hospital. Scrubs are easy enough to find, and I need the right costume for what I'm about to try. I change clothes in the attending doctor's bathroom. Then I change physically.

It's difficult, but when I focus I can change the melanin count in my skin. It's the hardest transformation for me. Nordeen says it's because my self-image is rooted in being black. I say it's because melanin is a hard substance to transmute. But I need to be less black to pull this off, so I focus until I can tell that I probably look mulatto. I close off my hair follicles and pull the thick mats that I have out and flush them down the toilet. Then I focus on slick black hair, coated in oil. I let it grow until I can fix a small rubber band at the base of my neck. Since I'm at a toilet I vomit up sixty-five pounds, making sure to check my discharge for too much stomach acids. I just need to lose the pounds, not my voice. When I step out I look like a sexy young intern that works too hard. I look at my watch. It's eleven. Almost time for lunch.

Chapter Eight

Catholic schoolgirl uniforms had to be designed by pedophiles. It's the only thing that makes sense. And that's the only partially normal thought in my head as I exit the tube and head for Atkins Road. This is Tamara's school. An all-girl's school. An all-girl's Catholic school where they're made to wear the pedophiles dream-uniform. Half a block away and I already smell the adolescent hormones. I try to respond in kind.

I did a lot of things on instinct during my cross-Africa trek that I later had to learn the specifics of. Keeping the animals from attacking me, for instance. In my delusional state, I thought it was simply because I was different. Over time I realized it had more to do with the manipulation of my scent. I call it stank. I sent out non-fear hormones. This confused the animals enough to make them leave me alone. Humans react to stank as well. It's obvious to me, but of course most people are unaware of which sensory input they are reacting to. We're a little more subtle about it than animals, but that person at work you can't stand? That girl whose number you just have to get? Stank. I read an article that said there's no evidence of pheromones existing. I really wish I could tell them about what I smell.

Teenagers are the worst. They reek of pheromones, like baby skunks that unleash all their odor at once, or adolescent rattlesnakes, full of venom. Human children spray their pheromones everywhere. Catholic schoolgirls are the worst of the worst.

I hit the playground exactly at noon, but I hold back a little bit, across the street from the bricked yard. The younger girls come out first. They go for balls and jump ropes. Then the older girls descend from their high tower of protection, hoping to take on whatever dangers the real world may have to offer. I keep my senses open for seared lungs. When I feel it, it comes from behind the playground, on the other end of the school. Makes sense. That's where the cool girls go to smoke. Tamara is either a cool girl or a freak. All of our kind are. We either lead the pseudo-outsiders, or we truly live the outsider experience. I'm banking on her mother's desire to make her "normal" affecting her enough to at least try for the outcast friends.

I take my time getting over to the girls but increase my perspiration rate and kick the "I'm sexy" hormones into overdrive. I'm making sure I'm downwind of the nuns, scared of what they'd do if they caught a whiff of me now.

"Any of you know a girl named Tamara?" I say, standing in front of five girls out of a bad eighties punk video. Two try to hide their cigarettes. Two take long drags and stand, looking at me with a scowl. One blushes. Girls respond to "I'm sexy" in different ways.

"Who wants to know?" A girl with a Southie accent. One day she'll be fat and bloated, like her mother; I can already feel a slower metabolism than normal. Which is why she smokes, so she doesn't have to eat and so she doesn't have to work off those calories. It's all unconscious for her, and that's what makes her the cause of stains on many teenage boy's sheets right now. But her cavity-ridden mouth and pockmarked face make her tough-girl impression almost laughable. Only I'm not playing games right now, so I give her the respect she thinks she wants. She doesn't realize she's standing so close, or that she's pressing down her skirt with her free hand, trying to make a good impression.

"Look, I'm not a cop, OK? I'm an intern down at the hospital. I know she's been missing for a while, but look, she's sick, OK? I can't say what. I've just got to find her."

"A bit much, the personal attention, enn'it?" the blushing one says, still not standing and not intrepid enough to look in my face. She'll grow to be gorgeous, provided she deals with the ulcer eating away at her intestines.

"We were . . . are . . . friends. I'm not trying to get her in trouble or anything, I promise. Look, if she's run away I won't tell anyone." Heart rates go through the roof on that one. Not sure what that means, but they're focusing on my words.

"You some kind of perv?" the second unabashed smoker is asking, leaning on her friend's shoulder, glaring hard, trying not to lick her lips. She tries for a posh accent, but her Brixton roots won't let her go. Although she's five shades lighter than me, even now with me at my lightest, one of her parents came from the Caribbean recently.

"Listen to me. She's sick. Really sick. But she doesn't know it. She could die. Plus, she's contagious. If you've seen her, if you shared drinks with her or ate from the same plate of food, you could be sick, too."

"How come the news hasn't said anything?" the blusher asks. She believes every word from my mouth.

"The news doesn't know. I'm sitting on it for as long as I can. Her father's a politician, and Tamara wouldn't want to be part of anything that would ruin his reputation. . . ."

"So, who's she to you, then?" Again, the brash smoker. Not as brash this time. Investigating. She wants to believe me.

"Like I said, we're . . . friends. She means a lot to me. She was acting weird before she disappeared. Came to the clinic where I work, all the time. We started talking, went for coffee. Oh God, I just realized how that sounds. I'm not attracted to her. I mean she's a beautiful girl, but I'm not . . ." They make my excuses for me, eating out of the palm of my hand. To them I'm a sexy but shy intern who's fallen in love with a girl too young for him. They'd kill their own mothers for me now.

"Awright, luv," unabashed Southie smoker says, patting my cheek. "We're all right here, yeah? An' none of ours been in spits breath of her since she disappeared yeah? But if you want to find her, it's that one over there, been looking at yaw since yaw come over here, yaw got to talk to, yeah?" She points past the park to the corner where I'd been standing. Another girl, not in uniform but around the same age, holds up a wall with her shoulder. She's frail, not more than one hundred and ten pounds, and dressed like she just raided the cool kid's store. Green button-up blouse, half-open, with a gray wifebeater underneath. She's wearing leggings of some sort, and a black trench coat three sizes too big for her. And she's got yellow sneakers that look like boxing shoes laced on to her feet. When she sees me looking, she starts walking away.

"You shouldn't smoke" is all I leave the Catholic girls with, taking the cigarette out of Ms. Brixton's mouth. I fix her asthma at the same time. I turn, marching toward my first real lead, suddenly feeling stupid in my scrubs.

When she rounds the corner, out of eyeshot, I reach for her body with my senses—and find an electrical storm in her brain. She's like me. I quit faking nonchalance and begin to run. I hit the corner hard and spot her at the end of the street. She's tensed and ready for a fight. Whatever she's got going doesn't block my skills. I could take her out in a second if I wanted to. But she knows where Yasmine's daughter is, so I play it smooth.

"I just want to talk," I say, closing the distance between us by half. Her respiration is through the roof. Her eyes are dilating. She's using her power. But not on me.

"What did you do?" Her voice betrays her youth. She can't be more than thirteen.

"Nothing. I'm just looking for a friend."

"You felt me. You touched me." The distance makes yelling the only way to communicate. I try to come forward, and she raises her hand. I'm half expecting fire or ice to flow from it. When nothing happens, I continue walking toward her.

"Yes. I did. I'm like you. Do you know Tamara?" Why are all the dogs in these houses barking?

"Stay away."

"I don't want to hurt you." Only a manhole cover separates her and me now. "I'm just looking for Tamara."

"Stay away from Tamara. She's ours now." She's trying to sound tough, but her fear is evident. But so is the squall of heat from her mind. I'm about to push her heart into calming down when I hear a window behind me shatter. I turn. A fucking dog, a big one. German shepherd. Big teeth, all showing. He's mad at me. I get it now. She talks to the animals.

I turn to face the girl. She's gone, but she's left a few dozen surprises. Rats the size of overweight cats swarm up from manhole covers with the same fury as the dog. Shit.

On instinct, I beef up my leg muscles, jump over the rats and away from the dog. For a second, I hope that the dog and the rats will get into it and leave me alone. Of course not. Three more windows break, and now there are four dogs. Great. Plus more rats every second. I hate rats. I hate little Pied-Piper-of-Hamlin girls that talk to rats and dogs. I run. No real strategy except to get to higher ground. I'm like a demented Dr. Doolittle, with a band of enraged house dogs and street rats forming a vicious tail behind me. Usually I'd just outrun them all. But I expended so much energy on my morphing that it's all I can do it keep the rabies babies from making a lunch out of my Achilles tendons. Since when do rats attack people? She does something to these animals. I'll figure it out after I get to surviving.

That may be harder than it sounds. Every second I have more enemies and fewer options. Ten dogs now. Can't count the seething mass of bouncing brown and black rodents. Too many. Is this how I go out, a feast for the vermin of London? I survived walking across Africa, damn it! Lions didn't touch me!

Right. Lions didn't touch me. I adjust my pheromones quickly, but I'm tired. Running, changing, Yasmine—too much in one day. I bump up my pheromones again, until I reek of predator, of the biggest, most vicious animal these city-dwelling creatures have ever had nightmares about. I'm what makes them want to grab their babies and run. I'm the biggest dog on the block.

By the time I round a corner into an abandoned construction site, my own face is back—I've got no energy to keep up the illusion—and I smell like Mr. Big Critter. But they just keep coming.

Somewhere nearby, that girl is still driving these creatures. They've slowed down, they're afraid of me—the pheromones. But she's pushing them to keep coming; I can feel their brains near seizing from her electrical storm.

I'm just about out of options. But not quite . . . someone's done me the solid of leaving a lead pipe here. I grab it. The first rat is a dead rat. The first dog is a wounded dog. After that, I can only promise I'll go down swinging. Too bad my powers don't work on animals. . . .

But they're not just animals, are they? This girl's got them on puppet strings. I can even feel them, through her. And if I can feel them, maybe I can hurt them. I reach out with my senses. Affecting them is going to be like trying to give a back massage with a catcher's mitt, but I think I can do it.

Fuck it. It's them or me. I raise my free hand and slam them all with my power. Half the rats die of heart attacks. Three of the dogs let out yelps of pain and spasm on the ground. I do it again. Another quarter of the rats go into spasm. Two dogs go down. If I were stronger, maybe . . . But I'm so tired. Some of the other animals scamper away. Not all. I use the last of my strength to beef up my muscle and reflexes, and bang the pipe against the outlines of a building that will never be constructed.

"Come on, you varmints!" Pathetic epithet, but it's all I've got. They come. I swing. Three rats first. I kick one back, stomp another's head, and dodge the third.

I guide the pipe into an arching swing, like I'm trying to reach deep left field. The blow tags the third rat in mid flight, and a German shepherd who just reached pipe's distance. Never seen a dog stagger before, but it couldn't come at a better time—he falls onto the mini army of rats that just reached the ankle-biting area. I take advantage of the reprieve and climb. The scaffolding behind me is all metal. There's a pit bull below me I don't want to figure out how to deal with. But the rats could get up here, if the girl didn't stop them. She's got them all huddled below me. And now I'm hearing her voice.

"You killed them!" she's bawling from the other end of the construction site. "What kind of man are you?"

"The kind that refuses to be eaten by animals!"

"They were just doing what I told them to do!"

"Then you're just as responsible for deaths as I am. Unless you want me to kill the rest of them, I suggest you call them off now." Pure bravado. Let's hope she can't read my mind.

"You're just as bad as her," the girl says, raising her hand. The animals disperse.

"Where's Tamara?"

"Whoever you are, whatever you really look like, you stay away from her. If you go near her, we'll kill you."

Now I've met twenty-one people like me.

Chapter Nine

I've had two days to recover from almost being eaten, and I still feel like five pounds of shit in a ten-pound bag. I've only woken up twice in those two days. Both times I ordered one of everything from room service, and devoured it all in under twenty minutes. Then hibernation again.

Sleeping for sixteen hours at a time should relax the mind. Not mine. All I could do was go over the entire fiasco and worry if I'd screwed things permanently. Maybe I'd failed, maybe I wasn't good enough. Maybe Yasmine was right. What the hell was I doing anyway? I'm no detective. I should just bail. Go back to . . .

Nordeen. He knows everything about people like us. Does he know about this? Is he laughing on his rooftop about his weak healer-slave, almost taken down by a little girl who talks to animals? I pray he's laughing. If he's upset, no place on earth is safe for me. I should call him, at least gain his counsel so he doesn't think I'm totally off the reservation.

But if he doesn't know anything, then I'm calling attention to myself. I'm giving him Yasmine and her daughter . . . if he doesn't have them already. Maybe this is part of his plan. He's got me. He knows he does. So he can send me out to attract more of us to his side, to whatever power game he's playing. That's his style. So if I call Nordeen, I truly fail.

So I lay in a near coma thinking on what went down. I start with the girl. Fifteen years old, at the most. Frail frame, racing blood pressure, well fed. Not homeless. Lots of silver rings on her hands, black leggings, dark green cinched blouse, black overcoat that makes her look like the lunatic-chic poster child. Not soldiered, not savvy. Had she gone in for the kill from jump, I'd be dead. But she also wasn't a student. The Catholic girls knew who she was, but she wasn't wearing a uniform, and it was school hours. So why was she there?

She knew her powers, but she used them like a club. There was no subtlety in her manipulation of the animals. They ran me up the scaffolding like a trapped fox, waiting at the base for fatigue to set in. If she'd called in other rats, they could've gotten me down. I'd have fallen. Game over. But she didn't. Instead she cried over the animals I'd already taken down. Not a soldier. She's weak in that way.

So a weak, non-soldier kid almost took me out. No. Wrong way to think about it. A weak, power-playing soldier scoped me investigating Tamara. This isn't about me. This is about Yasmine's girl. The girl who's missing but who still has someone peeping the school, with powers. Powered, non-soldier club kid scoping weeks after Tamara's disappeared. That's not covering tracks. That's looking. As far as I saw no MI5 or other government agents were posted. I could've missed them at first, but going after the girl in broad daylight would've attracted them to me. The government's given up on her, but this powered girl hasn't. Why?

That takes me through my first sixteen hours of sleep. While waiting for room service I shower, releasing every toxin my body's built up while I've been out. I want to call Yasmine, but what do I have to report?

I get the local papers delivered. Turn on the idiot box and watch for idiocy regarding Yasmine, Fish'n'Chips, or Tamara. Not sure if I'm relieved or saddened by the fact that there's nothing. It means I still get to be the hero. It also means I still have to do the work.

A knock at the door signals room service. Half the food is gone before the bellhop gets to the elevator. By the time he can brag about his fifty-quid tip, I'm near comatose again, wrestling with demons I'm only barely beginning to understand. I'm healed enough to function in the world but not enough to go up against the animal girl again. She's no soldier, but she's powerful. I have to go toe-to-toe with her again, there's going to be a body at the end of it. And I refuse to be taken out by a child. I don't care who she's working for.

And there's the insight. She said "We." She said, "If you go near her, *we'll* kill you." Not "I'll kill you." If she was talking about the dogs and rats she would've said "They'll kill you." It'd be more effective. But she said "We." I knew it all along, subconsciously. It's why I keep thinking of her as a soldier. Soldiers take orders, they don't think on their own. That's how animal girl was acting. Like she was doing what someone else told her. It's an organization. She's not alone.

Animal girl's comfortable enough with her powers to use them in broad daylight. So she's stupid, but she's also practiced. Practiced people like me don't take orders from norms. That means there's at least one other power. Probably more. If there are only two powers, why waste one on lookout for weeks? No, she's the weak link, the runt of the pack, assigned to the shit duty. That's how she carried herself. Wait. Why shit duty? Why was she waiting there? She wasn't waiting for me. She was looking for Tamara. Animal girl doesn't know where Tamara is. The "We" doesn't know where Tamara is. But they're looking.

Animal girl wanted me to think they knew where Tamara was. But if they did, why would they be scoping out the school? Why get into a confrontation? Why not just bring me to a secure spot and either show her to me or take me down?

Two reasons. They don't have her. And they don't know what they're doing. I'm not sure of the second reason. I can't get too cocky. This could be some subtle power play by a major player. Someone on Nordeen's scale, or higher. Tamara could be coveted by the grander powers and animal girl could just be another one in the power's grasp. I can't assume too much. All I know is that there is a "They" and they don't know where she is, either.

Not true. Animal girl said I was as bad as "her." Her biorhythm changed when she said it. She radiated fear, so much that it even blunted mine. At first I thought she was talking about Yasmine's girl. But I'm realizing the girl didn't have the same reaction when she said Tamara's name. There's another female. One that scares the animal girl. The boss. The boss is a girl, and she wants Tamara.

I wake up, and I'm famished yet again. I need to get out, change clothes, breathe non-air-conditioned air, walk more than twenty-five square feet. I pull a pack of Silk Cuts from a local candy vendor, and buy some of the dark brown paste that passes for chocolate. As a younger man, I took to smoking first to impress Yasmine, then stayed with it to test my self-healing. Since Morocco, it seems an effete use of my power; I've broken bones with the power of my mind and healed gaping cancerous holes with a touch. Clearing the nicotine out of my own lungs is too simple. But playing the Sam Spade role, even as ineffectively as I have been, makes me long for a cancer stick. Or maybe it's just the memories of London.

I was a younger man here. Someone who loved his woman, and who did the work of the righteous in secret. I felt like a super-hero when I put on my EMT uniform and covertly laid hands on. I bragged only to Yasmine, with a pride that would be the key of our undoing. But in my youthful ignorance, I felt complete here. I was quiet and special. Is there a way I can return to this peace? I've lost Yasmine, but if I find her daughter maybe . . . Or maybe even with another woman.

The moon reflects off the slick cobblestone streets on Lambeth Court, and I spy a red-haired woman in a bright green pencil dress and an old school Kangol. For a full minute I'm wanting her. I'm picturing us arm-in-arm, strolling the street together, about to meet up with a group of work friends at the local pub. Her bones tell me she's just thirty. Only five years younger than me. We could make it work.

I've got to talk to her. But when I step toward her, the razor around my neck bumps its edge against my chest. Nordeen.

I am his healer. His dog. I could have a family, but only if Mr. Maximus allowed it. I would live as Suleiman, at the beck and call of a shadow. I saw Nordeen holding Suleiman's youngest one time. The girl seemed fine. But I could feel Sulli's wife's sobs when the child was returned to her arms. No worse for wear, but the meaning was clear enough. Everything Suleiman had belonged to Nordeen.

I'm carrying my head low, turning away from the pencil dress, keeping an eye out for fashionably dressed club kids and rabid animals. I can't get out from under Nordeen. I made my deal with him. He didn't force me into it. He hasn't even threatened me since the day we met. Not overtly. But there's nothing I could gain for myself that he wouldn't have a piece of. My fantasy wife, life—shit, even my past—is owned by the mysterious shadow. The longer I'm in London, the more risk to Yasmine and Tamara. Better to find the girl and leave before Nordeen catches wind of what's happening. Shit, it may already be too late.

I call Yasmine and try not to sound too disenchanted.

"Hello?"

"Mene?"

"Tag. Have you . . ."

"Not over the phone."

"Fine. Wait. Are you OK?"

"What do you mean?"

"It's two-twenty in the morning. Are you hurt?"

"I don't get hurt, remember? At least not . . ." I'm halfway through the sentence before I realize how much I'll sound like a pansy if I complete it.

"I've got an appointment from seven to nine. Can we say ten?"

"Where?"

"Do you know the Fox Club?"

"I can find it."

"Good. And Tag?"

"Yeah, Mene?"

"Be . . . yourself. Please?" I hang up because I'm too happy.

No one calls me Tag. And she didn't protest when I called her by the old name. Plus, she wants to see my face. No food could fill me up the way she just did. I can't sleep.

It's seven in the morning, and after two bad movies and one gigantic breakfast I'm calling down for a tailor. I'm liking these all-inclusive hotels. So long as you have the money you can have anything delivered to your room at any time of day. I ask the tailor to bring up five of his best suits. I change in the bathroom as he waits in the bedroom, astounded by the amount of empty room-service plates in the room. I try each suit on for size, then adjust my body modestly to fill it out the best way I can. Reverse tailoring. I only let the groggy-eyed Armenian suitsmith me in the suit I like the most, a cream-colored doubled-breasted number that narrows at the hips, almost like a zoot suit. He's astounded to find it fits like a glove.

I ask him for five more pairs of slacks and a few button-up shirts before sending him on his way. He's way too happy about the one hundred euro tip. If I run into him again, I'll fix his strained eyes. Another call secures a cab. The tube would just muddy this suit; a limo would be too much, and I don't like the idea of being tied to a car in London. Shit. It's only eight-thirty.

The cabbie, a Jamaican by way of Cambridge if his fake accent is to be the indicator, knows the Fox Club. He peeps me in the rearview and nods in approval. It's the black man nod, a currency only valued in situations where black people aren't the majority. I haven't seen it in so long it takes me a second to realize why his eyes shine so brightly. I guess not a lot of his Fox Club fares are black.

I'm half an hour early. I ask the fake Jamaican to drive around the block a few times, after paying him double what's on the meter.

He smiles and asks if he should wait for me to return from the club. I'm tempted. Instead I get out when the once around the block eats up fifteen minutes. I tip him again, and he asks if I'm sure I don't want him to stay. I smile politely, press down the suit, and enter the narrow doors.

If the rich and elite of the international crowd ever organized youth hostels, it would look like this place. Shit. I picked the best suit the tailor had, and I still feel underdressed. The hostess is a leggy, black-haired woman with a round face and the abysmal teeth Brits are known for. She asks if I'm a member.

"He's with me, Barbara." Yasmine is a business-suited angel, coming to save me from embarrassment. She strolls across the main floor, her hand dancing along the full-length zinc bar with such a casual air that by the time she's by me, the hostess already feels calmer. "I should've told you I was expecting a guest, but I just wasn't sure this was the man coming."

"No problem, Mrs. Bridgecombe. So sorry for all your troubles these days."

"Sweet of you to say." Yasmine's grip bites into my arm, punctuating the girl's comment. I'm still savoring her touch. Squeeze all you want. "Can you send a breakfast plate to the club room?" She doesn't wait for an answer. No one could tell she was pissed. No one but me.

"Silly tart," she says in a volume designed for two. "She doesn't care one bit about Tamara. Or me, for that matter."

"Mrs. Bridgecombe?" is all I can muster.

"I am married, Tag. It would be unseemly for me to retain my maiden name. . . ."

"I know." I didn't. "It's just weird to hear." She sits me in a room too large for only two people. The remnants of her earlier meeting are still present. An organizational charity event, apparently. She makes a phone call and does some straightening up until the breakfast plate arrives. She directs the server to place it directly in front of me, still talking into the phone. I feel awkward. I want this damn suit off. This is where Yasmine went when I went across the globe. It's natural for her to be in this environment. I'm still trying to figure out my nature.

As soon as she's off the phone, Yasmine is putting on music, classical, one notch too loud. No one will complain once she closes the door, but I fail to see the point of it. When she unbuttons her blouse to reveal those two perfect breasts, held back by a thin black bra, I get my first involuntary erection in years.

"Feel free to eat it all. My meeting was a breakfast meeting. I remember that you get hungry whenever you do your thing. As you can see, I'm not wearing a wire. If you need me to totally disrobe, I will—so long as you promise to keep your hands to yourself."

"Why would you be wearing a wire?"

"I wouldn't. But you were so concerned about your anonymity before, I wanted to prove to you that I took your concerns seriously."

"I believe you." I'm still having hard time looking at her eyes. "Thank you."

"If you want to thank me . . ." Shit. The tears. They're falling down like all her defenses. "Tell me you found my daughter." It was all an act. The poise, the confidence, the courtesy, the breakfast meeting. None of it means shit to her. All she wants is her daughter. My boner embarrasses me. Still, I don't dare move closer to her. I can see her breasts, and she's crying. It was how she won every argument we ever had in college. We'd end up in bed together whispering apologies until we fell asleep. But that was a lifetime ago.

I give her what I have, and she goes stoic. Not angry or even upset. The tears end. But her top stays open—out of neglect, not enticement. As soon as I talk about visiting the school, the animal girl, nothing else matters. Even the parts of my story where I'm in danger don't garner so much as a mock gasp of concern. Barbara the hostess would've given more feigned sympathy. Yasmine just listens, staring at the marrow in my skull, trying to decipher the meaning of my story—which admittedly sounds insane in the retelling.

I give her my theories as just that, theories, leaving out the "what if a grander power is at play" parts. If it's true, there's nothing we can do about it, and we'll know soon enough. I think I'm done three times before I finally stop talking. She offers a cigarette, and I take one with no intention of smoking it.

I half expect her to light her smoke the old-fashioned way, with her power. The lighter in her hand triggers a sadness I don't feel like demonstrating. She kills the smoke before speaking.

"If these others are after her, why run?" I can barely hear the question over the music, but I nod as the words hit my ears. It's a good question.

"She loves you. She loves her father. Someone knows what you love, they can control you."

"You think this animal girl and her friends would threaten me, threaten Darren?"

"From what you say about your daughter, that would be the only way to get her to disappear from you."

"But you say they don't have her?" She flashes the first real smile I've seen from her in a while.

"She's smart. She buried herself so deep somewhere, no one can find her. Not government, not this animal girl and her friends—"

"Not you?" Didn't know a question could bite and be honest at the same time.

"Not yet. I've done this before, things like this. Plus I know London.

"Not like she does." No pride this time, just a sinking into the depressive blanket that's been covering her since her girl took off. "Darren never let her out too late, but she has friends that I've seen. Partiers. We used to call them ravers. I don't think that's in fashion anymore, Tag. Raving. But she knows this generation's equivalent. The city is not the same as when we were younger."

"She's a star among candles. Pretty soon someone's going to see her light."

"Find her." She grabs for my hand and holds it tight between both of hers.

"I will." I'm begging inside that she never lets go. When she does, I guess my face shows a little too much.

"What?"

"Nothing."

"I shouldn't have touched you." She stands, beginning to button her blouse again. The music is dying out.

"It's OK."

"No, I shouldn't have."

"No." I'm angry as I stand to meet her eyes. "I know I'm just a freak on a mission." I'm expecting another slap, a tear, something to show she remembers breaking my heart. Instead I get a sideways shrug, and her back as she strolls over to change the music.

The food came with mimosas. I pour a champagne-heavy one, thinking how nice it would be to reduce my alcohol tolerance and make myself useless to her. Her narrow chin is hanging open, laden with a prepared speech when she returns to her chair. She crosses her legs like a lady of the highest court and asks me to sit with her eyes. Despite my aerial view of her now buttoned-up breasts, I comply.

"When I left you, I was young. I wasn't sure what was pushing me away from you. The easiest thing to point to was the thing you do. But six years ago, when you had that note delivered to me, and when I heard about what could've only been you trekking across Africa— hell, whenever I heard anything that sounded like your name—I had to think about the truth. I figured it out a while ago. It seemed too inconsequential to call you over. It didn't change how I felt about you. Didn't change the fact that I was married with a beautiful daughter, doing what I always wanted to do. So I left you alone. But you came when I called. You say you don't want my money. I respect that. But can I give you this knowledge as some form of payment for what you've done, and what you've committed to doing?"

I don't answer, and she takes that as permission to continue.

"It wasn't the healing. I'm sorry that I made you believe that it was. Oddly enough, me calling you a freak was my way of trying to be compassionate. The truth is, I left because of you. My god, Taggert, think of what you could have been doing with your power. Even under cover you could've applied to medical school; even nursing I would've understood. But instead you drove around London in an ambulance, always volunteering for the most dangerous shifts in the most disastrous neighborhoods—and for what? Just to see if you could survive it? You thought I didn't want to hear your stories when you came home because they *bored* me? Taggert, you terrified me every night. I was constantly afraid you'd never come home. I understand the concept of necessary risk. But your risk was reckless. How could I think of marrying you, or starting a family with you, when you lived in harm's way for no other purpose than it excited you? Taggert, I left because I didn't want to see you die. I should have said that, I know. But I was young, and you were scaring me. I thought maybe it had something to do with what happened with your brother. I thought maybe the guilt over—"

"If you want to see your daughter again, I suggest you shut your fucking mouth." I say it the calmest voice I can. I'm rageful. And no part of me regrets it. I won't touch her. Not ever. In any way. Again. I'm standing and walking over to the window to get away from her petrified stare. She didn't know what I could do, how hard I could go. She does now. Bitch.

I'm miles away from her now, though I'm standing on the porch. She brought up Mac. She's the only one I ever told about him. Nordeen didn't know about him until I gave it up as a price for my sabbatical. She brought him up. She says I feel guilty about him. But she doesn't feel guilty about breaking my heart with a letter? For calling me a freak, for throwing me away and then pulling me back when she needs me? There's guilt, but it's not mine. There are no words for what I want to do to her.

All of a sudden, she's behind me. Her arms wrapped tight around my waist from behind. I can feel her half-melon-sized breasts resting on my back, loose again, and I wonder if I could grow hands and a tongue on my back just to recapture what I lost all those years ago. When did she unbutton her shirt?

"If you want, I'll sleep with you," she says, trying to sound like the idea doesn't disgust her. She's terrified of me right now. "It would have to be now, here. But if that's what it takes—"

"To find Tamara." I turn on her, getting those dangerous feelings of comfort off of me. "It would be a labor, a kindness to an old friend doing you a favor." We both know that's all she's offering.

"I'm married," she musters. "But if it will keep you to the task, I don't care. I promise I'll be good. I won't—"

"Stop it." I storm back into the huge room, heading for the music. It's all too confusing. I miss my rooftop.

"You promised you'd find her," Yasmine screams and then is surprised that she did. I turn the music off. "I didn't mean to make you angry. I'm sorry. I swear, Taggert, I didn't mean to upset you."

She's shaking in nervous panic. She's got no reserves left. This is the cost of my rage. She's seen it before in my eyes. She knows what my vengeance looks like and wants no part of it. This isn't ire, it's panic. Her breasts are heaving and falling quicker than California tectonic plates. She lets out that squeal that only dogs can hear. It's the one sound she hates making. Right before she falls on her knees I'm there. I catch her before those perfect knees hit this hardwood floor. I catch her before she falls. I always will. I pull her close to my chest.

It's George Washington University again. We're in college, and she's telling me about the first time she set a fire with her mind and how scary it is, and even though I can't relate because I love using my power I pull her close to me, up under my skin, so she can be as close to my heart as nature and physics will allow. She's that close.

"Find my baby," I think she sobs in my ear.

"I swear I will." And that's when Fish'n'Chips walks in.

*

The ridiculous look on his face, the doofy smile, the suit almost too small for his overextended arms, and his odd long head make him too cartoonish to take seriously. Until the bastard walks directly up to me and swings at my jaw. What's more, he connects.

"Son of a bitch," I sputter. Shock, more than anything, makes me let go of Yasmine before I hit the floor. The pasty-faced white boy works out. Cartilage under his knuckles shows he's been in a fight or two before. Not like the one he's about to be in.

"Darren!" Yasmine shouts at her man before looking down and seeing her breasts flowing free in the wind. Her embarrassment is evident, but I don't care.

I stand and outstretch my hand. He's saying something while looking at Yasmine. His face is already apologetic. Can't hear. Rage has clouded my ears. Now he's allergic to his own body. His throat is closing up. His usually pasty skin is going beet red. Hit me? Faggot-ass nonpowered bitch of a politician. I can heal gods! What the fuck can you do? I cloud his eyes with hay-fever tears and start the muscle spasms brought on by excessive coughing in under thirty seconds. I'm about to infect his heart with some stray bacteria from his intestines when my coat catches on fire.

Yasmine stands in front of me angry and pleading. She's a walking contradiction. I still can't hear. A fucking norm thought he could get away with touching me. I'm seeing her begging. She thinks the burning jacket will stop me. I can heal from burning. The insult from Fish'n'Chips will take a little bit. Still, the smell of burning flesh, the instinctual closing off of nerves so I won't feel my skin merging with the cotton and nylon in my new suit shirt and jacket, shock me back into reality. I let her man go and give Yasmine the eye.

"Nothing ever could hurt me. Except you." I walk outside the room, jacket smoking, to face government boys with weapons half drawn. Of course. They go where he goes. I want to scream. Instead I put my hands on my head with fingers interlocked.

Chapter Ten

Yasmine is good with her tongue. In less than five minutes she's explained away the burnt jacket as a candle mishap and somehow gotten her man to chill out on finding her with me, her blouse half opened while mimosas and bad classical music set the mood. It works for her man, but that's not me. Not anymore. I've had guns pulled on me, my brother has been mentioned, and I've been punched by Fish'n'Chips. None of these facts bode well for the rest of my day.

"I owe you an apology," Darren is offering in the government luxury sedan, which is just one promotion away from being a limousine. He extends a hand to me. Behind me in the front section I feel the passenger security–detail man flinch slightly. He hasn't cleared me with security yet, doesn't think his mark should be touching me.

"I'd probably have reacted the same way." I take his hand as I lie to him. He's got the beginnings of prostate trouble. I'm taking some juvenile pleasure in knowing the man Yasmine picked over me is going to need to have a finger stuck up his ass sometime soon. It should be funnier. But I'm nervous and I don't know why. It's not the guns, not the hit in the jaw, not Yasmine trying to set me on fire. It's something else. A slow burn

"It was just that she hadn't mentioned it to me, you understand. So when security called me and reported that a strange man was meeting with her, I jumped to conclusions."

"I didn't want to raise your hopes." She's perched below him just like she used to be with me. "What's the sense in raising your hopes if he can't find anything?"

"So you're a private investigator?" His eyes haven't left me. I'm realizing he's not a totally unattractive man for a Brit. Far paler than milk, but he's well toned, a condition not so much of working out with any consistency but a diet of coffee and the stray vegetables Yasmine pushes in his way—at least if his stomach has anything to say about it. His angled jaw holds that classic, working-class pride which makes the idea of digging ditches seem so noble.

I'm noticing all of this, but its just distraction. There's something else going on—near us, around us. Yasmine's body notices even if her mind doesn't.

"How're you feeling?" I ask. He's a norm. I don't feel obliged to maintain Yasmine's lies to him, not when she's displaying her domesticated fervor with no regard to me.

"Yes, honey," she interjects smoothly. "That allergy attack you had earlier must have been hell on your system." I can't help but smile a little bit.

"That was the most curious thing," he says, finally breaking his gaze to loosen his collar. "And right on the heels of making an ass of myself with your friend. I'm sorry, I didn't catch your name."

"Do you feel it?" There's an electrical storm happening in a nearby brain. Yasmine knows I'm talking to her. It's our sort of "it." The "it" I'd see in her eyes whenever she saw fire, like a master violinist approaching a Stradivarius, the "it" she was in my eyes whenever I came home from work.

"Feel what?"

"Quiet, Fish'n'Chips," I snap.

"What?" Yasmine is concerned. Her body is reacting, stomach tensing, her brain attuning itself to whatever foreign signals flames offer. Somewhere, something is burning. It's close by, but I don't see it. I'm scanning the windows, both sides of the car, trying not to look frantic and failing miserably.

"Someone like me. Close by." I'm trying to keep my voice down. The security in the front already doesn't like me.

"What's going on?" Darren is getting scared. One hand is already wrapped tightly around the oh-shit grip above the door.

"Be quiet, love," she says more tenderly than I thought those words could be delivered. "Is it the girl with the animals?"

"No. Someone different. Bigger." I'm feeling a buildup of pressure somewhere close; it matches the rising of the mental storm. I try and pinpoint it. I scan Yasmine, her man, the security people. Nothing. It's another body, close, focusing power on us. "We've got to get out of the car. Now!"

"But why?" Darren's asking.

"Trust us, honey," Yasmine says, tapping on the soundproof glass that separates the front section from us. As soon as it comes down she speaks. "Stop the car. We need to get out."

The security detail argues all the bullshit reasons we can't pull over, but I'm feeling this swelling like an impact wound that fills with blood before the blow is complete. Only I can't find the body. I jump to the left of the car, scanning outside for anyone, anything about to . . . explode violently. You try and find someone ready to blow, then tell me what they look like. I slide to the right of the car, ignoring Fish'n'Chips's confused gaze. The Thames is just as murky as the sky, traffic is phenomenally slow, young and old Britons alike make their way through the fall afternoon bundled against the coming cold. Again, nothing unusual. I'm desperate, but I can't locate it. All I know is that soon this blister is going to pop. It's not going to pop on a body. I'd feel it if it were any of our bodies. It's not a matter of flesh. But the buildup is coming from somewhere. I stop focusing on my powers and analyze the situation logically. A second too late.

"Oh God. Mene?" I'm crying.

"Tag?" That's all she can say. It's the gas tank. My nickname is the last word that escapes her lips before the car blows. Times like this, I wish blacking out was easier for me. Instead I get to watch the gas tank push metal, flame, and seat up through Darren. It happens in under a second, but my perception gets precise and detailed under stressful conditions, so I witness the macabre cartoon of Fish'n'Chips's demise like it was on Blu-ray. He's flattening against the roof of the car before even it gives way to the heat. Mene . . . Her arm is gone, along with the rest of her right side, engulfed in flame by the time I have a chance to look in her direction. I want to scream, but when I open my mouth the fire finds an opening and sears from my throat to my belly quicker than I can heal. I get relief of a sort. The force of the explosion propels me through the front of the car, past the cab, and into the street. My back scrapes the engine block, immovable but inferno hot. Through it all, I'm still reaching for Yasmine. I have to stay conscious. Instinctively, my body tries to regrow skin first. Wrong move. My lungs and internal tissue are more important right now. I'll redraw eyelids and other facial features later. I'm still conscious to see the secondary explosion of the car.

The two guards in the front seat never knew what hit them. No weapons drawn. No attempt to get out. Only screaming and clawing at their own skin, trying to get the pieces of glass out of their eyes. I can't hear them. The explosion destroyed my eardrums. That's why I'm stumbling, why I almost impale myself on a flaming metal spike thrown up from the trunk of the car.

I take a break from making new pink lungs to redraw my eardrums. That means I also take a break from shutting down my pain receptors. I have to know what balance feels like. I feel it all for a second and understand the value of painkillers as I never have before. Fuck. The car blew up.

We're on one of the bridges over the Thames. I can't tell which one. I can't shut my eyes. I have no eyelids, and just melted flesh where there used to be a skinny face, and half my throat is gone. A piece of metal from my seat is lodged in my back. All I can really see is the modern-art piece that used to be the car . I'm pulling myself through the still-flaming debris. I see the upper part of Yasmine's arm and grab it instinctually. The car, body parts, norms—we're all scattered across the street. I move a melted piece of engine and realize that it was half-merged with Yasmine's hip. She doesn't scream. She's too far gone. I can see skull. I scream my pain and hers. It wakes her for a second.

"Baby!" She's still alive. I can heal her.

"Oh God, oh God . . ." She's talking with absolutely no control over her lower jaw. It's dislocated, maybe broken as well.

"You're fine. I've got you. You're with me now. I can heal you. . . ." Three of her ribs are stabbing into her pancreas, her lungs, and her spleen. She's literally burned to the bone over most of the right side of her body. Both her legs are gone. I can't stop her organ systems from failing. Her jaw is dislocated. I should've eaten more.

"Oh God, Darren. He . . . Is he . . .?" I want to laugh; she almost sounds drunk. I want this to be a mistake, a joke, anything other than a successful assassination attempt. I'm regretting my world, all my time away from her, coming back, meeting her, sharing that first cigarette in college. I wish I'd never met her, wish there was some way that this wouldn't hurt so much.

"I can't do anything for him, Mene. Sit down . . . No, Yasmine, don't move. I'm trying to heal you." My power is limited. The thing inside me won't let me heal her, because it's too busy healing me. I'm trying. I'm pushing, but it's like the powers don't think I can do anything. For all my control, it is still the thing that lives inside me that does the work. And it, not me, has decided my life is more important than hers. But I can—

"Where's my daughter?" I can't heal, but I can still sense. I've felt this before. This is death. Death hates me. Just like everyone else. Death wants me. When it realizes it can't have me, that my lungs are already healed, that I'm working on my esophagus now, that soon my skin will be coming back, when it realizes this it targets my reason for living. She coughs blood in my face. A message from death. The poorest people in Africa told me a healer is death to a warrior's spirit. But they don't know what death is to me. Death is my ultimate enemy, and given enough time, death always wins.

"I'll find her, Yasmine. I'll find her. I'll protect her. I promise . . ." She's gone. There's nothing in this bag of flesh that I know anymore. It's just a collection of elements, mostly water and blood, calcium deposits, nerve clusters . . . there is no more Mene. I want to curl up next to her, be under her like she was under me back at G.W. late at night, listening to Liz Phair, a lifetime ago. But there's something ugly and dark inside me that knows to run when it hears sirens. The rest of the world starts demanding attention. It's all broken cars, people, and screams. Nothing on the bridge remains whole after the explosion. I am not fully featured yet. I have only the stubs of eyelids. I'm missing a face. My clothes are half burned off me. But I run. I run down by the Thames. And out of some perverse need to cleanse myself of my sins I am yet to commit, I consecrate my body to the water. I baptize myself in the Thames and do not reemerge.

Chapter Eleven

Yasmine is dead. My organs are fully healed, but I am not. I smell of the waste of London. I am famished, half naked in half-burnt clothes. Someone tried to kill me and ended up hitting the only woman I've ever loved. They made a big mistake.

I wait until nighttime, part out of design and part out of lack of energy. I cause a drunk young neo-Nazi, about my weight and size and walking alone, to pass out near me. I take him down to the river and strip him of his leathers, his boots, his jacket, and his shirt. Fuck him. He's got sixty quid in his pocket. I find the nearest curry stand and demand five orders of tikka masala and butter chicken. I'm done in five minutes. I think about ordering more but then realize that my face still looks like a half-baked pizza.

The concierge and the rest of the staff look at me funny when I finally get back to the hotel. I've grown enough of a face back after the masala to not care anymore. I'm crying in the elevator. I'm crying in my room. I'm crying in the shower. I'm crying ordering room service. Four suits are resting on the bed. Near twenty-four hours ago, I left this room fresh-pressed to impress the woman I thought wanted me again. I hate the suits. My tears don't stop when the bell-hop arrives with the food. I tip him. He doesn't bother to ask what's wrong. I thank him mentally for that privacy. I gorge myself, then pass out on the floor. Beds are for people that don't watch their true loves die.

I'm awake. Maybe it was a dream. I'm starving again, and my facial skin is two-toned. My lungs are as clean as a baby's. That means I did have to do the healing. Which means I was in a car that blew up. Which means Yasmine is gone. I'm bawling again. I turn on the TV, more to drown out my own sobs than any quest for entertainment. Of course it's the big story. Not because of Yasmine, but for Fish'n'Chips. They've spun it to be—hell, maybe they actually believe it is—a plot by terrorists against the current administration. Politicians are running wild. They say the car was hit with "as yet unidentified explosives." Speculations include road bombs and ICBM's. They don't know. I know. Someone like me hit us. Someone who can make things explode. I felt their brain focusing on us right before . . .

I'll find this power. And when I do, I'll kill them. No. I'll make their ribs go through their spines; I'll make a wired mess of their spinal cord. I'll make them allergic to their own blood. Then I'll kill them.

But I can't yet. I don't know where to find them. What's more, the public nature of this thing—it isn't what we do. People like me, we go under the radar. We don't attract attention unless we're ready to square off with the norms *and* all the other powers that don't want the attention. People like me don't do that. Sane people like me don't. The kid in India, his powers had made him crazy. I've met three others like that: a girl in Singapore who jumped between dreams and was unable to distinguish between the dream world and this one; another girl in Ankara who found everything she touched, including her parents, turned to liquid; and a third in Garoua, Cameroon, whose body was in constant flux, shifting its physical characteristics based on the desires of the people around it. Nordeen had me cull them all, and I was thankful that was his order.

But the one who killed my Yasmine wasn't crazy. Whoever they are, they're sane enough to work with the animal girl. The animal girl was a street kid, hungry, desperate, scared out of her mind, but not crazy. And if I'm right about the animal girl being subordinate, that means the one who caused the fuel in the car to blow is superior to her, maybe the one calling the shots. So they're not crazy, they're just bold. Bold can mean stupid, or it can mean backed up by an even larger power. A power unafraid of killing a semi-famous politician and another power in broad-ass daylight.

I'm killing the asshole either way. But I've got to know which way the wind is blowing. I tried to go mellow on this one, tried to keep it all away from the boss. But that's not the way it's destined to go down. He's going to know about this. Hell, it's on the BBC. Maybe he was always going to know and I was just deluding myself. But I've got this much control over the situation: I can call him.

I'm half dressed in a clean suit, one that makes me feel like I'm going to a funeral, when it hits me. I held her severed arm in my hand. I forced the snags and sinews of bone back into place and made marrow and red blood vessels rejoin, but it was no good. Yasmine is dead. She'll never come back. I can't heal her. I thought I could handle it.

I'm throwing up. I just make it to the bathroom, the tub. Succumbing to involuntary, unconscious physiological activity brands me as weak, distracted, not on my game. It's the first surprise my body has given me in years. I'm bawling without making a sound. Before my powers, when Mac used to beat me, this is how I cried in my closet when he was done, just so I wouldn't disturb anyone else. That's not the concern now. I just don't know any other way to cry. I don't know how to stop, either.

Figure it out. Focus on death. That feeling of pull that shut down each of my broken girl's systems, when all I could do was watch. I couldn't break free of her, couldn't let her face the darkness by herself. I know in the end she didn't love me. I was a poor substitute for her massacred man. Didn't matter. I couldn't let her go. So I felt her brain shut down; I suffered her heart pumping as she bled out. I sensed her lungs pulling in blood and mucus and marrow—futile and useless bags of organs not capable of saving her. Just like me. Her pull on my arm, weak already, went limp, and I felt the lack of electrical impulse in her body. I didn't just feel it; I recorded each and every sensation. I can replicate each one. I will. I'll play it back plus ten for the bastard that caused my love to fall. And before they go down, I'll wet concrete with their brain matter. I'll explode their marrow out of their bones and make a mess of capillaries. I'll make a paste of their eyes, Yasmine, I promise. I'll make them bleed from their ears and turn their digestive system against them. They'll digest their own organs. I'll increase their pain receptors so that their clothes feel like sandpaper. I'll make their own breath sound like a DC-10 is landing in their chest. I'll fill their lungs with every excessive fluid in their body I can find. I'll make a decomposing mess of them, I swear I will. They'll pray to gods they don't believe in for the pain to end before I explode each taste bud in their mouth and inflame their genitals with the stray parasites their immune system usually fights off.

Nordeen said the best I could hope for would be to at one point be of assistance to a god. He's wrong. I'll turn into a god of pain and disease, and build an altar to you from the bones of your murderer. Their suffering will be my first odes, and they will not end until I feel satisfied that even dead, resting wherever you are resting, you can hear the pain of the idiot that thought your death would go unavenged. In the end I'll make their skin like taffy and pull it across a full city block and set fire to it. Even then I won't let them go unconscious, let alone die. They will feel what you felt; cry as you were too strong to do, beg for the death that already claimed you. And when they can take no more, I'll heal them completely and totally. I'll take every moment of pain and suffering from their body. I'll make them feel better than they ever have in their life. I'll give them that peace for a full minute. Then I'll tear them apart, cell by cell again until there is absolutely nothing left for them to do but kill themselves. And then, when they've put themselves out of their misery, then I'll find your little girl and let her know her mother's killer has truly suffered for what they did.

I'm calm now, replete with purpose. I make my way downstairs and to the nearest bus. I ride it to Essex. It takes a while. I'm overdressed for the bus. Luckily I'm carrying the "Fuck with me" look in my eye, so even the drunk kids with their singsong neighborhood patois leave me alone. I get off the bus with an hour to spare before the bars close. I find a hopping club. The Black Dog. Perfect. It's how I feel. I order a drink, and in under a minute I've pilfered a cell phone from a chav woman's purse hanging off her chair. Everyone's drunk. Nobody cares. I dial eight different international codes from memory. I'm beginning to think I screwed one up when, after half an hour of waiting, it finally rings.

"Speak." It's Suleiman. He's speaking in Arabic. I used the hash wholesale number we have.

"It's me," I say in French.

"There are many me's in the world. Give me a name or I lose the connection," Suleiman responds in deadpan French.

"The Godfather to your second child shouldn't have to identify himself." I wait for a second and interpret this silence as acceptance. "I need to speak to our big brother."

"At this number?" His voice is full with as much happiness as he'll ever allow on the phone, and I miss my old life. It feels like a distant shore getting smaller and smaller.

"If it's tonight. If not, I'll call from another number in thirty-six hours." When he's confident I won't say anything else, the consummate professional hangs up. Somehow, I can feel his concern.

I set the phone to vibrate, then hide it deep in my pocket. Finally, it's back to the bar, where I demand a Black and Tan with a double shot of Jameson to start off. I want to kill off my body's ability to process alcohol. I want to feel drunk. I want to wreck my system. If not for the call in to Nordeen, I would. But the small razor sitting on my chest seems to burn when I think about it, and I know whose property I am.

Norm life, drinks at a bar with the mates, trying to pick up some fit girl—it doesn't usually bother me. I'll admit to a private jealousy when I see the tourists in Marrakesh or Moulay Idriss holding hands with their children, casual. The norms don't know, can't perceive the world around them the way I can. They don't see the old powers in the darkness, the ones that make such grand machinations and movements that they seem predestined. Usually, I envy such innocence. But not tonight. Tonight I'm on a murder mission. That means someone is going to die. Most likely it will be the idiot that tried to make a kabob out of me. But I'd be a moron if I didn't realize that whoever angled in on me almost took me out with his last attempt.

Times like this, I don't wish for ignorance. I look around and I see the bloated ignorance of the lumpen proletariat: roly-poly, sausage-fingered, ginger-topped fathers of at least two illegitimate children trying to massage the asses of waiflike, peroxide-scarred students who are themselves trying to navigate adulthood with their new-found freedom from outdated parenting. Luckily, booze makes it all seem rational, or at the very least palatable. This was the world that would have been mine had Yasmine not . . . What? Died? Left me? Rejected her power? Married poor dumb Fish'n'Chips? I want to honor the dead and pretend that this life of pubs and anorexic waitresses would have been fine for me. After all, even Fish'n'Chips's NGO circles are just champagne versions of the larger party I'm watching now. In truth, all permutations of this life bore me. Yasmine got it wrong. She thought I was chasing death when I was searching out wisdom. I beg for all the knowledge in the world. But I'm in this for the death right now. So I order another of the same before the last call sneaks in on me. Two minutes later, the stolen phone in my pocket vibrates.

"After all you've been through, I would've expected a better outing from you." Nordeen's voice is paper thin, with more timber than bass. Still, he's not angry, which relieves me of a small part of my anxiety about calling him.

"I didn't know what I was dealing with," I'm saying, walking away from the bar into the back patio. "Your last words to me have been proven false."

"I believe I said we tend to stay away from each other for good reasons. Are you now saying we all tend to stay close to each other?"

"Maybe just those of us in London," I say, taking a swig. No use even trying to hide where I am from him anymore. Most likely he knew where I was going all along. If not, my calling from a random cell phone with an Essex callback would be all he needs to figure it out.

"London is much like Marseilles now, though its security can be seen as much more benevolent, according to some." There's a familiar acridity in his voice, though I can't place when I've heard it before.

"Could that benevolence be behind what I've been going through?"

"The motivations of the mover in those regions are a mystery to most, even myself. It claims one motivation but will often act in ways that seem contraindicated."

"You're losing me."

"Never," he says, way too sharply.

"I mean I'm not understanding you." I'm trying to muster supplication, but it's hard with the vision of dead Yasmine going through my mind.

"Then come home. This is a poor medium for truth-based conversation. Your mission has ended tragically, true, but it is over."

"I still owe the ones who did the deed payback." I want to scream my protest to him, want to tell him how I'll kill them. "But I'm concerned about crossing greater powers, including you."

"Your reason for staying is solely to settle this debt?" Only a few days away, and I've forgotten the danger of his questions.

"Like you said, a poor medium we're on. I don't want to return until I fulfill an old friend's final request." I don't want to bring Tamara too much to his attention.

"Then we shall have to find a better medium, yes?" He hangs up before I can respond. The call is so confusing I chuck the phone over the back wall of the patio and into someone's bird pond five units over. I'm out the bar with the rest of the early quitters.

I take a cab back. The cabby's a Nigerian. After offering me weed, stolen jewelry, and khat, he settles his eyes on the road and leaves me to his dubbed version of "Dark Side of the Moon." Fucking Nordeen. He knew where I was. He knew about the explosion. Hell, half of the world knows about it. He knew I was dealing with powers. He knew it all and told me nothing. I'm ready to move. I think I can track the exploder down. I know I can find the dog girl again. I just need one of them. I bet the boss knows where both of them are. I don't know what he wants. I can't find a better medium. He's like a petulant god, demanding offerings but not revealing what foods or spices he enjoys. I lost more than I gained by calling him and should have expected as much. The cabbie overcharges me for my return to the hotel. I pay the inflated charge and reactivate his oral and genital herpes as a tip.

I'm completely ignoring the lobby when the concierge politely asks for my attention.

"This was hand-delivered for you about half an hour ago, sir." It's a small envelope with a black-encrusted razor on the front. Nordeen.

"Hand-delivered?"

"Yes, sir."

"By who?"

"I would say a normal delivery person."

"And would you happen to remember the height of this normal delivery person?"

"Height, sir?"

"Yes, height, or age, race, at this point I'd even settle for gender. Do you know if it was a man or woman that delivered this letter for me at 12:45 a.m.?" I shouldn't be castigating this sad norm.

"I'm sorry, sir. It's been a long night. I can honestly say I don't remember. If it's important, I can check our video logs to—"

"Forget it." I don't even bother looking at the letter again until I'm alone in the elevator. A black jeweled razor across the front of the envelope. Big deal. Maybe it is from Nordeen. Or maybe it's from somebody who knows I work for him. Either way, someone found me. Either way, someone wants me to do something. In this line of work, you only send letters when you want something. Wanting something's not an issue. If it's not Nordeen and they want something from me, the answer is "no" . . . assuming the request has nothing to do with finding Yasmine's killer.

I'm more concerned that another power like me was at my hotel. I've passively scanned everyone I've come across here for the ability to turn an electrical storm on in their brain, and gotten nothing. But the letter means that someone who knows I work for Nordeen is looking for me. I'm opening my room door with my keycard, wondering if this is how all those other powers felt when Nordeen sent me to them.

The door is closed before I realize there's someone in my room. I'm sloppy. Tired. I turn to look behind me and get hit with a wave of pure force. No hand could deliver this blow. It doesn't just hit me—it sweeps the room, pushing everything twenty feet forward. For a moment, I panic. The last time I felt someone "push" me this powerfully it was my brother. But I look ahead, brace for the impact into the wall, and see that, it, too, has been pushed forward and ripped from the rest of the building like a stray plank off a wooden ship caught in a typhoon. It's not Mac. My brother would never let pass the opportunity to push me hard against a wall. Good. Not Mac. Now, how do I deal with being pushed out over the street by a massive invisible wave?

Chapter Twelve

I am so sick of powers that I don't know trying to kill me. But I'll survive being pushed out of my thirtieth-floor room if for no other reason than to prove that it'll take a lot more than that for these assholes to kill me.

Looking down, I see that the ground—the pavement, the people, the cars, all of them—are moving laterally, not getting bigger. That means I'm not exactly falling yet. I've got this.

My assassin is powerful and stupid, or, more likely, untrained. If you have the power to push all the contents of a room twenty feet forward, then you could've just done that to my head.

Flight equals height, propulsion, and trajectory. I wrap my arms together tightly and arch my back and aim for the office building. The main pieces of my room wall are still traveling outward before me; they weigh at least three times as much as I do. That means if I do nothing, I'll fly at least as far as they do. I look down again. Fuck, I'm up high. Fuck that. Focus. Aim your body. The idiot behind you put a lot into that one blow. Let it be their downfall.

The wall debris is halfway across the street before it starts to fall. Good. Across the street, the windows of the business building have shattered. Blessings. Just aim. Arch your back, you stupid bastard. Toughen the skin, compact the bones, deaden the epidermal nerves. This will only hurt if you . . . landing is going to be rough. Curl, the office floor will be carpeted. Arch your damn back. Fist in front, in case of computers and big machinery. Here it comes.

I land like a spastic chicken. Almost forget to dodge the lighter contents of my room until some of them embed themselves in the walls over here. Fuck. Whoever it is, they're strong. And looking across for me. The lights are out. Smart little twat. I can feel their eyes strain. Fuck it, you little bastard. You want to see me? No problem.

I brush the loose bits of glass and shattered metal off my body. I boost my adrenal output, kick up my ATP to Olympic runner stats, and dense up my leg muscles so tight they're almost bulletproof.

"Wrong day to fuck with wrong man." And I run. I run at the gaping hole in the side of the building, the hole in my life, the hole in my future if I screw this. I'm powered by rage and a weird bio-chemical prowess that makes people like me special, a process that give us abilities no one truly understands but one for which we will be hunted and killed anyway. I run with my weird fuel, and just when it looks like I'm doing what Yasmine always thought I would, I jump instead. I'm sailing across the night sky again, angry, heading at the yawning expanse created not five seconds ago. Halfway there, I see my unsuspecting foe. This moron is dressed in all black, complete with a lower mouth cover. Can't be more than fifteen years old. Doesn't matter. Dog girl taught me what happens when I underestimate kids. Before this kid can process my crazy ass flying across the street, I've got a super dense fist going straight into that masked jaw. The punk does good. At the last minute he pushes back against my fist with the same power that pushed me out the window. Instinct saved the jaw. Won't save this asshole. I'm dropping my knees on the fuckwit's ribs, making them more brittle with my power. I saw cops in the distance on my jump back over. I won't have a lot of time to get this done.

"I am tired of you little fuckers trying to kill me!" I grab the bastard by the neck and drag him into the bathroom. Fire alarms are going off. The hotel is emptying. I don't care. I keep his head in the toilet with my foot. All of a sudden I'm flooded with images of Mac again.

He hates me. I'm little again, in our house in Maryland. I'm only eight. He throws me into the ceiling and pins me to the floor with his power. It's the first time I've seen him use his power so blatantly. He says he's better than I ever will be and that I should worship him. Oh God!

What's going on?

My skin is tearing. Ants and beetles fat with blood are crawling out my skin. They've lived in my body all my life. I am the sum of their thoughts. I'm in the burning car with Yasmine.

I am the burning.

Her skin is melting off, and I'm sitting next to her. Smiling. No.

In between waves of guilt and nausea, I realize I've felt this before. I am not seeing ants and fires. I'm feeling them. My visual cortex is picking up nothing, and my frontal cortex is in overdrive. I keep reminding myself to pay attention to my body, like Nordeen has taught me. This has happened before.

Guinea a couple of years ago. Local witchdoctor with real power, but thought he was a match for Nordeen. He threatened to steal our souls. Instead he did . . . what's happening to me now, forcing emotions and sensations on me, demanding that my mind come up with some logic as to why my skin feels like it's bleeding off, why I'm freezing and sweating at the same time. It's like a bad acid trip. I stopped it then, and I can stop this now.

I lash out. I cause all bodies in a six-foot radius of me to shut down renal functions. I demylinate all neurons in under a second. It's not out of choice—I just reach out with my powers and pull. It stops the images. Fucking telepath. This wannabe ninja is a telepath, and a girl if my powers are any judge. But my opponent has her head out of the toilet. Her nose is bleeding, her brain is seizing. Her blood is building up toxic levels of waste by the second. She's still got hate in her eyes.

"You killed my parents." Fuck! Tamara. Dressed like a goddamn ninja, I should've known. Telekinetic and telepathic. I heal her quickly but keep her energy low. She's powerful and angry. That's dangerous.

"I'm saying this once. I don't have time to convince you, and after what you just did I'm sure as hell not letting you in my head. My name is Taggert. I am . . . was . . . a friend of your mother's."

"Such a friend you killed her!" The rage in her posh accent, turned hard by street living, is almost endearing—like a rabid fox snapping out of fear more than aggression.

"Use your head for something other than a hat rack, girl. What kind of killer sits in the car he's rigged with explosives?" It's a logic she can't fight, but I boost her pulse rate and clear her headache a little, just so she can think clearly. I'm famished and freezing lying against this tub. "You were just in my head, right? You pulled . . . you saw what I saw. Any part of that even seem like fun to me?"

"You could be her." She stands, trying to figure out how to get the embarrassment of toilet water out of her hair.

"Who?"

"Or work for her."

"Unlike you, I don't read minds. Feel like trying to make some sense?"

"What do you want from me?" She's looking down at me, eyes still filled with tears, but now more born of frustration than anything else. My back is getting cold. That's a bad sign for me. Means my body is so tired from the jump, the fight, and the neurotoxins Tamara flooded my brain with that it's not up for maintenance healings. No way I'm letting this little girl know that.

"She wanted me to find you." She knows what I'm talking about. I let my words sit in the air until she admits her own fatigue and sits on the sink. "Now I want to find the assholes that killed her. I get the sense you can help me with that. You down?"

"You're like us?"

"Us?"

"Me and Mum . . ." She starts choking on her tears.

"No time. I'm sorry I shoved your head in the toilet, but you've got to decide pretty quick if you trust me. Cops are coming. . . ." I don't need to go on. She shouldn't be able to stand after the beating I gave her. Even with my healing. But the notion of cops has her moving. I stand to match her eyes only to find she's a good foot and a half shorter than me. "So, do you trust me?"

"You say your name is Taggert." I nod. "My mum says she only ever told one person what she could do with her powers. What—"

"She could set fires. Put them out, too. I accidentally lit some curtains in a cabin when we first knew each other, and she put them out. That's how—"

"OK. You're him. What now?"

The girl's got power. We leave the room and no one sees us. She won't let them. I'm stumbling a little, looking like a drunk, but no one is noticing the barrel-chested swarthy guy with glass in his hair or the toilet-smelling ninja as we walk by. At first I thought it was the alarms distracting them, but I spot-check the cornea of one of the people running by us to get to the stairs, and we're not even a blip on his visual cortex. Firemen and cops run past us, baffled by the reports from their comrades already in my old suite. They want to know how a window wall can be blown out without a hint of fire damage or evidence of explosives. At least they think they want to know.

Outside, thoroughly confused Britons gawk at the sky, and the little girl in all black keeps her mental miasma up. I see one or two people trying to stare at us, but only for a second. I don't know what they see, and neither do they. But somewhere in their minds, Tamara gets them to decide it's not worth remembering or focusing on. The contents of a hotel room from thirty stories above make much more interesting observation. I take an extra second to scan for wounded and find none. Good. I take Tamara's hand and let her guide me.

I'm thinking we're going for a car. Either hers, or a stolen one, or even a taxi. Instead she angles for the Underground, which makes no sense because the damn thing is closed. But she's moving with purpose, and I'm not in the mood to argue. I can barely keep my eyes open I'm so tired and hungry. In the station she hops down quickly onto the tracks and starts jogging. I adjust my eyes to the lack of light and follow quickly behind her. Ten minutes of sharp turns and descents down elevator shafts and we end up in what used to be a tube stop—the type often forgotten by maps and city dwellers alike. It's cemented up. The girl stands back, breathes deep like she's about to do some heavy lifting, then pushes a five-by-three section of cement straight back. She doesn't glow, doesn't hum, but I feel the explosion in her mind that only our kind can produce. The only sounds are a slight grunting from her and the giving of the ground beneath her feet as some invisible power pushes her backward slightly. Throughout our night jog I've paid attention to the rats, which seemed to care nothing for us or the empty trains that roar above, behind, and to the sides of us. But all creatures back away from Tamara as she uses her power. She's strong. But she's also tired. I almost don't make it to her side to catch her when she falls from exhaustion. I smell rosewater in her hair as I gather her up in my arms, gently. A perfect square of orange light heralds us into the station.

Inside, the old station is clean and dry. More than that, it looks like a kid's room. There's a stereo, a laptop, running water, even a bathtub. The pictures on the wall—the crown prince and other pop stars—don't match with the girl I'm holding in my arms, but what do I know about interior design and teenagers? Tamara's fighting for consciousness. I give her body the cue to sleep, and it thanks me. There's a huge futon, unmade, in the center of the station. I take off her shoes. I put her in the futon and tuck her in. I unwrap her hair from the yard-long black cloth that's been holding it hostage since our fight. That deep eggplant red/black combination puts me in mind of her mother, especially with the rosewater. She looks like the kid pictures I've seen of Yasmine.

I go over to the mini fridge. Sodas and water. I drink three of both, then sit on the pavement at the foot of the futon. In my pocket, the razor letter. Why not? Nothing else can shock me today. I tear it open with my fingers. Just an address. In Cheswick.

There's a twinkle in my mind, a foreign storm in my port, and I'm awake. I know where I am, who I am, and how I got here—just not how I fell asleep. So I don't lash out. And as soon as I'm fully awake, the alien storm has an eye. Tamara is standing over me, hands on her hips, shoulder-length black/red hair pulled to one side. Her face wears the battle scars of shock and exhaustion poorly. She's got creases where her cheekbones, jaw, and eye sockets should be smooth. I try not to take pity on her.

"So, you fly?" she's demanding.

"No. I jumped. How'd you find this place?" I stand and do the stretches I know will kick my natural body chemistry into gear. I pay attention to the pains and aches in my body the way mechanics pay attention to the pings and vibrations in their cars. Every pain, or lack thereof, tells me something. By the stiffness in my legs I can tell I've been asleep for at least three hours.

"Friend. Former friend, she used to squat here. I saw it when she wasn't looking and took it over when she left. What do you do?" She's trying to sound more London than she is. Either that or the posh schoolgirl enunciation of Yasmine's was a lie.

"I heal. What kind of friend?"

"The kind I'm going to kill the next time I see." I stop stretching and take a deep look in her eyes. She wants to mean it. She wants to be that hardcore, but she's not.

"The one who lived here, that the one that made the car explode?"

"No. Explain the healing thing."

"Answer my question first."

"Why?"

"Because I'm older and smarter than you, and I don't want you getting the idea that we're equals." She clears the distance between us in under a second.

"Get it straight, old man. I talked to the girls at school—who said you looked different than you do now, by the way. I caught you meeting up with mum at the club. I tracked you down. I snuck into your room, I gave you the impromptu flying lesson, and you're hiding in my spot. So, yeah, we're not equals. I'm better than you."

"Put down whatever it is you're smoking, child, and start thinking. You tracked me down? I was hired to find you. If you couldn't find me, then I wouldn't have been doing my job. Trust, I don't want to be found, I won't be. I'll give you credit for getting the drop on me, but all you did with that advantage was give me time to strike back. If I hadn't put together who you were, your face would still be in that toilet bowl. You're powerful, but you obviously have little training and even less skill. Save your attitude for the norms, because you're just not that impressive to me." She's so confused by the calm I'm exuding, the calm I'm making her feel, that she has to break the closeness she established. She searches the fridge before speaking again. I'm sitting on the corner of her bed.

"Drink up the whole icebox why don't you?"

"Side effect of my power, I'm afraid. I get thirsty and hungry often. Now, who lived here before you?"

"Her name is Prentis," she says after she realizes I won't let the subject go. "She can talk to animals. Rats and dogs mostly . . ."

"We've met."

"Alia sent her after you, did she?" She says that name with all the venom in her throat. Alia.

"This Prentis works for Alia?"

"More like Prentis is her dog. Prentis was on the street most of her life. Living with her pets like she was one of them. Years before I ever linked up with her, Alia found her. I don't know the right word for what she did to her. . . ."

"Does it involve powers?"

"No. I mean maybe, but I don't think so. What do you call it when one person crushes another's will solely by influence?"

"Slavery?" I'm asking.

"Then it's like Prentis is her slave, but Alia never laid a glove on her, so I don't know . . ."

"Who is this Alia?"

"She's the reason I'm hiding out in Prentis's old squat. You want the guy who blew up the car . . ." She's pausing, breathing deep to control her tears. When she speaks again there's a slight quiver in her voice. "I want Alia. She's the boss."

"You know who took out the car?"

"His name's Rajesh. He's Alia's muscle. He would've been my first suspect if not for you showing up and tailing Mum . . ."

"And they're all like us?"

"I'm nothing like—"

"What I mean is, they all have powers, right?" She nods her head. "Tell me what you know about them. Tell me everything."

She sits down on her bed before she starts. Tamara may be slumming it, but she crosses her legs and has diction that is to the manor born when necessary. Still, as I look at her, I'm hard-pressed to find Fish'n'Chips. Yasmine is written in her deep olive skin, oval face, and dark red hair. She is my former lover's child through and through. Her mother used to adopt the same posture whenever she had serious information to give, poised and legs crossed, but relaxed.

To steady her nerves, or to make the point that she's grown, Tamara fishes a pack of smokes out of somewhere and lights one without offering me anything but her suspicion.

"Prentis was like a known street kid, yeah? She never talked about parents or home, yaw know? Everybody knew her but she's what, maybe a year younger than me? So when she wanted to hang, I just

accepted it. She was like this instant street cred, yeah? This is beginning of last form, last year. I didn't know she could do the thing with
the animals. I just thought she was just good with dogs and stuff, see?
Like she'd talk to them and they'd do what she said. It was just a thing.

"I kept her away from Mom and Dad. I knew, I fucking knew they
wouldn't approve of her. She's sweet, least I thought she was, but she
was always dirty. Not in her head, yeah? Like physically. Maybe from
living down here, don't know. Guess that wasn't really the issue. It was
more that she was always scared. I didn't think of her as anything more
than a cool accessory-type friend. I should feel bad about it, but . . .

"'Bout three weeks after we start hanging out, I start getting these
headaches, yeah? I'm catching echoes from sounds that aren't really
there. I'm getting nosebleeds that only are relieved when I focus on
something. So I'm concentrating more on not blinking than on my
iPhone, and what happens? Thing goes flying across the room. The
iPhone, I'm saying. I do it again to prove I'm not crazy, then take it
down to Prentis, yeah? Figured she's street level, knows things. So I
show her the trick. And then she shows me hers. Says there's someone
who knows a lot more about this stuff than she does . . ."

"Alia." I fill in the blank.

"Purebred cunt." She almost spits. "Didn't think so at the time,
you know. She looked cool, profiled like a retired movie star at age
sixteen. Like she knew everything. Ran an underground club, too.
Every other Tuesday and Friday. Bender, it's called. It's someplace
new every time, right? Sometimes abandoned cinemas, sometimes
posh houses. Doesn't matter. It's always packed. Always the dopest
scenesters. I didn't really believe Prentis when she said she knew Alia.
I'd heard of Bender, and Prentis *was* cool but just seemed under the
radar. But sure enough, she walked me right into this warehouse over
in Dagenham and introduced us all proper like. Alia said she was
from Brighton, moved up a couple of years ago, but even then I could
tell something was off. . . ."

"What can she do?"

"She's everything you don't see." The girl said it like it was supposed to shock me. "Me, I can do the thing I did to get us out of your hotel. I can blend in to the background of what people are thinking, yeah? They can look right at me but not see me, if I want. If I focus hard I can do what I did to you in the bathroom, like just pull up everything in a person's head, all the muck and mire of it. More often than not I just catch strong stray thoughts from folks. Alia, she's a surgeon in the mind. She crafts images complete with emotion, texture, all of it. She can make you feel, see, taste, touch, or hear anything she wants you to. Truth is, I don't really know what she looks like. She's always looking like someone new."

"So how did you hang out with her?"

"Shit, like I wanted to? I was more down for Prentis. Felt bad for her, you know?"

"Why?"

"At the time she hadn't been responsible for any badness, yeah? Plus, I don't know, the way Alia talked about her, to her, made me feel more like the girl was her dog than anything."

"What did Alia want from you?"

"Wanted me to tell her everything about my thing, you know? She got off on seeing it. Kept asking me how I felt when I used it. If I believed in God, the devil, all the typical overdramatic teenage shit. I would've marked her as mad if it hadn't been for the Bender parties."

"How's that?"

"Well, yeah, she was nutty around me, but everyone kept talking about how cool Bender was and how everyone wanted to be close to Alia and all that. Here I was trying to gain distance from her—"

"Yeah, but why? I don't know teenage-girl talk, so when you say she was nutty around you, I don't really know what that means." She thinks for a while, considering her words for the first time. Her guard is down, and I'm seeing a little beauty that's going to turn into a great one in time, if the tragedy of her parent's death, or possibly her own, doesn't overwhelm her.

"It's like she wanted to go lesbian with me but just kiss," she says after a few moments of silence. "Had a girl in school not too long ago like that. Not my thing. Not against it, but the girl kept following me, telling me how special I was. Realizing now it might be part of my power, yeah? But back then it was right nutter. Alia never tried to make a move, but she's—like blacks say in America—'all in my grill.'"

"I've never said that in my life." She's questioning with her eyes when I realize she doesn't know I'm an American. "Keep talking, though. I understand."

"Not much to tell, really. I kept hanging with Prentis for a while. But she started pressuring me to kick it with Alia. I wasn't feeling it, so I'd bounce. A couple of weeks ago, just to shut Prentis up, I agree to meet them for dinner at this curry spot in White Chapel. That's where I meet Rajesh." It takes me a second to put it together.

"He blew up the car." I'm still trying to keep my voice flat, emotionless. But now it's clear I'm trying.

"That's his power. He focuses on something for a half a second and it explodes. He's Asian, Paki, I think. I don't know—he could be an Afghan. It was his parent's spot we ate at. He sat us in the back of the restaurant, and before I finished my vindaloo he made a few of the empty bowls around us explode. Alia said that the three of them were forming a union of people like us. That we should be running things, not just keeping our skills to ourselves."

"What did you think about the idea?"

"Well, I'm here now, aren't I?" She gets up, angry. I want to say something, but I feel her jaw relaxing and her throat clearing so I stay quiet. "I mean, shit, it would've been easier to just go along with them, yeah? Probably what I should've done. I didn't tell Mum everything, but I told her enough so that even she knew it was a bad idea to be around them anymore. So I stalled for time. I told them I was thinking about it. I even started going to Bender more often so Alia wouldn't get too suspicious. But Rajesh, he just kept pressuring, saying I was either for or against them, right? I'm all 'What, I can't be neutral?' And he's all 'For what we've got planned, there is no neutral.' They started threatening Mum and Da. I knew Da couldn't even have a hint of this type of thing around his career."

"So you left." I nod in approval.

"But how do you hide from someone who could look like anyone else, sound like anyone else?" the girl says, finally feeling like she had someone who could understand where she was at.

"You hide in plain view." I open my hands to indicate her current abode. "No animal droppings or scent in here for some time—means Prentis hadn't lived here for a while. Maybe not since this Alia found her, took her in, made the girl *her* dog."

"Yeah." Tamara is surprised. "Prentis never took me here. Only described it to me. Told me she'd been by her 'old place' and it was bricked up. I took note 'cause it was the only time she ever spoke about having a place to stay. Peeked in her head, almost by accident, to see where it was. Are you a real detective?"

"I've done this before. I've chased down people like us before."

"For what cause?" I'm uncomfortable answering the question so I don't. She doesn't let it go. "What do you do for a living, Taggert?"

"I work for a man that makes Alia look like the punk child she is. I'm not important here. You are. Tell me the rest. They threaten, you run. Then what?"

"Nothing. I stay low, trying to figure out my next plan, and they couldn't find me. There was no need to do anything until . . ."

"I showed up." Now it's my turn to stand and pace.

"I don't blame you," she says quickly. "I mean I did at first when I thought maybe you worked for Alia. But I know who you are. Mom never told me, but she thought of you often. I'd catch traces in her mind. Images of you two together, happy. That's why, once I saw your face, I wasn't scared of you . . ." She stops talking, and I realize I've got tears. Damn it.

"She thought of me often?" The girl nods her head. She wants to step close to me, but I back away before she can. Water across my face just masks the tears. But even that helps. "Tell me about this Rajesh."

"He's a bully." She spits for real this time. "A big stupid Paki bastard bully. He pushes his parents around. I've heard he's raped girls. Prentis never admitted it, but I'm sure he's raped her. He doesn't just blow things up—he likes to break things. People, souls, possessions— don't matter so long as he sees it break. I always hated him. I think Alia brought him out to intimidate me. You sit across from him, knowing what he does, what he can do, means you're sitting across from a loaded gun. He told me one time he made a man's head explode just because he saw it in an old movie. The man hadn't done anything. He was just sitting in his own living room, minding his own business, and Rajesh could see him and so he made the old man's head explode. He's a savage fucking brute who you can't take unless you grab him by surprise because if he knows you're coming he'll explode your heart and then rape you." It takes her seconds to say it all. Huge, saucer-like pupils have taken the place of the bullet holes Tamara usually has for eyes. Her pulse is through the roof, her lungs feel like they're running a marathon, and there's a massive buildup of carbon monoxide in her blood. She's getting hysterical. There're better ways to do this, but I don't know how.

"They didn't suffer. Your dad didn't even know what hit him. I cut off your mom's pain centers before I crawled back to her." It's a necessary lie. Nothing is holding her tears back now. I haven't done this since her mother and I were together; I haven't been called upon to comfort anyone. That's not Nordeen business. I hold the girl in my arms, tight. She sobs and beats against my chest. She screams those inarticulate sounds you can only make when you've lost everything. She empties it all into my chest and mind. While her hands are clawing at my wrecked button-up, her mind is unconsciously trolling mine for a sense of comfort connected with her parents. It's not intentional or malicious, it's just what baby psychics do.

In a sense I'm envious that she can still hurt so deep. But I can't let her into my hurt places. She can't see what I am, or what I may have to do. So I set up my white wall of defense in my mind as gently as I can. It makes her feel alone again, cut off from anyone who could understand her. So she wails on me viciously, sobbing, knowing it's all unfair. And I let her. She breaks the hold some ten minutes after the crying begins. But I don't let her go totally. I hold the back of her elbows so she can't gain much distance.

"We've got to put this pain away right now, OK? Fuckers that did this have to pay. They're powerful, but they're not very smart. Me and you have to use our brains. That means emotions get put someplace else right now, you with me?" She nods. "And let's get it clear now. Rajesh is mine. I know you want him gone, but that bastard blew up the car with me in it. I know you loved your parents, but he made it personal on me. Plus, I made a promise to your mother. So that blood debt is mine. The other two I'll help you track down. You get to decide what to do with them. If you've got a killer's stomach, and that's your leaning, I won't try and put you against your nature."

"I'm only fourteen," she says trying to pull away from me. I'm not letting her.

"Not anymore. This is your blood rite. You'll never be 'only' anything again. You're . . ."

"But you called Alia a punk child."

"That girl hides behind masks and uses rapist emissaries to get people on her side. You take the responsibility of your family's safety on yourself and gain distance."

"For all the good it did."

"You don't have control over the world, Tamara. Only yourself. And what did you do when you thought I was the one that hit your parents? You came for blood. So stop acting like this Alia bitch is someone to be feared. You're the one standing tall while she's lurking in the shadows. Why do you think she was recruiting so hard? She wanted your strength." It's only when the girl nods slowly, contemplatively, that I let her go.

We don't talk for a bit. She puts her headphones on. Not out of disrespect—it's just the way she thinks. She's been through a lot, and I don't have a clear plan yet, so I give her space.

There's not much to do in a walled-up tube station. I go to the other end and check my body. I find a metal bar braced above the stairs that currently lead nowhere and decide to do some pull-ups. I exercise for the sake of it. Push-ups. Normal. Upside down. One-handed. Clapping. Sit-ups. Regular. Upside down. Left-oriented. Right-oriented. It's all a distraction. I could get the same effects with my mind. But this way I can stop feeling her severed arm in my hand. I can stop hearing the explosion. It's okay I can let the images, the sensations, go. I've got a new fuel for my rage. A name. Rajesh.

I'm grunting upside down, half tranced out, when Tamara approaches me. My biological clock tells me two hours have passed.

"There's something I don't understand." She's genuinely confused. I don't stop my upside-down sit-ups. "What can you do? I mean, what is your—"

"I told you. I'm a healer," I say on instinct. "I play bodies like a musician plays his instrument."

"But you said you worked for a man that made Alia seem like some punk kid."

"What's your point?"

"And you said you've tracked down people like us before."

"I'm still waiting for your point."

"It didn't sound like you tracked them down to heal them." My trance is gone. So is my exercise. I unhook my legs from the bar.

"Best healers are the ones who know how to hurt" is all I'll say. I'm ready now. I've got a plan. At least, enough of one to get me away from the hard questions this kid has only taken two hours to get to. She's following behind me, a little too close. She must have sealed up her entrance to this place when I was asleep. "I need you to let me out of here and seal yourself back in."

"Where are you going?" Genuine panic.

"Remember that boss? Well, he sent me an invitation that I can't ignore." She's given me authority enough to not clock my eyes on a regular. If she did, or if her mind started straying into mine like it did before, I might not be able to hide what I suspect about Nordeen . . . or what I felt for her mother.

"But what about all that 'taking Alia down' talk?" I've got to flood her system with dopamine just to counteract the adrenaline she's pumping through her blood. She calms down a little. A little.

"It's all true. I've just got to make sure he's not involved with your girl in any way."

"And if he is?" Damn good question. I reach in my pocket and pull out my remaining cash. Thirty thousand quid. I take one thousand off of it and throw the rest on her bed.

"If he's involved that means I've got to go through him. I may not walk out of that one. So if I don't come back within 24 hours, take that cash and leave London. Fuck it, leave the UK. Stay out of Marseilles, Malaysia, and, Morocco while you're at it."

"Any other M place I should cross off my running-scared list?"

"This isn't a fucking joke, Tamara."

"The fuck it's not! You say it's me and you versus Alia and her people, but first you've got to check in with your boss and make sure it's OK with him? And, what, if he says no then forget the whole deal and just start running? Sounds pretty queer to me."

"Girl, I have purposely kept this man's name from you so that if you ever encounter him—"

"Nordeen Maximus." Shit! She's a better mind reader than I thought. Fuck! I didn't even feel her in my head. I try not to break concentration.

"I was trying to keep his name from you so that you could claim ignorance about him. If you know anything about him, he treats you like a threat. And trust when I say you don't want him in your life at all. You don't know him."

"He doesn't know me." Fair point, but the passive telepathy makes her dangerous. She's the type Nordeen would have me take out. But she is Mene's daughter, full of the same fire and drive as her mother. I will not let him get her.

"Point made," I say, going over to the money. I face all the bills again and try and hand it to her. "This is the way it goes."

"This is the way you want it to go." I'm ignoring that one.

"Without trust, we've got nothing. Smartest thing you've done since this all started was disappear. I'm not you. Smartest thing I can do is make sure my feet are one hundred percent clean before tracking more mud through your already disheveled house."

"What the fuck does that mean?"

"It means give me twelve hours. I'm not back by that time, I've got no call to tell you what to do with your life. My hope is that you'll run. But you want to use this money for a vengeance parade, I've nothing to say about it." She looks confused. "For fuck sake, girl, I'm giving you thirty thousand quid to do the same thing you've already been doing. You've brains, OK? Wicked smart girl who has instincts for days. Your instinct said hide and you did, right? Well, just stay hidden."

"I don't want your money!" She's yelling and crying at the same time. The dopamine has worn off. "I want the fuckers who killed my parents." For the second time in under a day, I hold her. Her body responds like it's what she wanted all along, someone sturdy and strong to rely on. But that's not me. That's her father she wishes she was holding, a man I couldn't be bothered to remember the name of. I'm standing in for someone I hated, trying to be a better man than I can be. This can't end well if I play the way I usually do.

"Me, too," I say in hushed tones. "But I want you to survive the experience. I'm begging you, Tamara. Just give me twelve hours."

"There's no food." Don't think I've ever heard a teenager whine like that before.

"Six hours. Grab some food as soon as I leave. I'll be back in six hours and we'll plan.

"Or you won't."

"Or I won't."

Chapter Thirteen

I'm heading the opposite direction as Tamara in the tube, following human heartbeats to find my way out. She can secure food. I keep telling myself that over and over. As I angle past small-monkey-sized rats and other nonhuman denizens of London's deep, I'm convincing myself I know what I'm doing leaving a traumatized fourteen-year-old alone. She survived just fine without me. She knows the city.

I'm worried for her. I'm having a hard time finding my way back up to surface streets, and I'm scared she'll get caught, that this Alia will find her and she'll never make it back to the cement cave. The fact that this is running through my mind as I'm on my way to pick up Nordeen's more appropriate conduit for communication—or a trap by one of Nordeen's enemies-—tells me a lot about myself.

I see the light of a station a few feet head of me, and I'm already missing the cement cave, the fiction of it, that it blocks us off from the rest of the world. I really like that little girl. And I feel for her. I'll protect her for as long as I can. So long as this Alia isn't protected from on high, I'm confident I can take her. It's early morning, and the station only has three people in it. I wait until all their eyes are fixed on the train coming in on the other side of the tracks before I jump onto the platform. I make sure to avoid the ever-present cameras as I make my way up to the street, the dark, gray, cold street.

I'll handle this Alia. Then I'll disappear from Tamara's life. If I take too much of an interest in her, the boss will get curious. If he gets curious he'll want to meet her. And if he meets her . . .

I step out under a drizzling sky. Me with no raincoat or umbrella. Suspicious. I've got to find a cheap clothing store. I've got to change, and I've got to get to this address the boss provided. I don't have a lot of time. There's a little girl waiting on me. It's only when I walk into the department store that I see people looking at me sheepishly. I feel the tightness on my face, the rise in my jaw muscles. I'm smiling. Fuck.

Ten minutes from West Kensington, and I'm convinced everyone is staring at me. It's not the smile. I lost that half an hour ago when I went to the mega-mart for some normal-looking clothes. When going to speak with Nordeen, smiles are not appropriate. What's more, they make him curious. He's the only man I hear say "Why is he so happy?" and think he's making a threat. So the smile is lost. But I'm still gaining attention in this neighborhood.

It's a growing immigrant neighborhood. When I lived in London, these families probably lived in the council estates. Now, by saving their money from selling whatever it was they could—gum, news-papers, their home, food, questionable driving abilities—they can afford modest homes not too far from their old stomping grounds. From the tube to the address, I'm getting stares from kids in turbans to old women in sarongs. Soccer games stop, chins are scratched, eyes lock on me. I'm wearing jeans with a casual hoodie over a button-up, topped off with a dark tan overcoat. My face and features are stable. It's not like they've never had foot traffic in this neighborhood. It's making me nervous. Is this Alia? Another power? Is this how Nordeen plans to do me in, through paranoia?

I'm waiting at the door of the address on the card. I'm almost afraid to knock. But there's a little girl hiding behind cement blocks for me. She needs me. That's a good feeling. Shit, I'm smiling again. That's when the door opens.

"You?" she says. It's the Ethiopian, the tiny girl Nordeen asked me to deliver to the metronome-hearted East Ender the last time I was in London. She stands before me, older and wrapped in thick white cloth save for one shoulder. There is nothing but surprise in her face. I forgot how beautiful she is. Before, she was a child, not much older than Tamara. Now she seems my age, with a knowledge of the world in her eyes that matches mine.

"I mean you no harm." Whether she believes me or not, she makes no move. I give her the card that was delivered to me. "I was directed here."

"Your master is more devious than even I thought possible. He picks his only servant who has done me no harm to collect his debt. Enter and be welcome, healer."

Her little Victorian matches her demeanor. It speaks in layers. The couches and other furniture are strictly old-world Ethiopian, created by a master craftsman schooled in ebony woodwork. Every cushion is covered in a base cream-colored cloth with a bright contrast slash in either red, blue, or green cutting across it at an angle that makes my head hurt if I look at it for too long. But instead of big-headed biblical tales as posters like most of her orthodox Christian country folk, she has Tibetan flag paintings of demons, posters of Tupac, and huge canvas hand paintings of apocalyptic visions directly on the walls. I see creatures that look like humans in that they have arms, legs, and hands coalescing from dust in the middle of impressionist representations of what can only be human souls. All the souls are running to join another sepia-toned amorphous creature, larger than the threatening, humanlike creatures. The humans are forming the body of their protector. It's like a mandala. There's more and more detail the longer I look at it. So I turn away, in case it's an elaborate distraction.

There's some insane world beat music on. Not the hippy kind—this is music spun by a dj obviously trying to work something out.

It's raw, complicated, no 4/4s anywhere near it. But it's disciplined enough for even the most unskilled dancer to find a groove in. Wait a minute . . . Where the hell are the speakers?

The house is traditional and futuristic at the same time. It's so unnerving I refuse to sit until she comes back with a tray of tea. She's taken her hood down to reveal five small cornrows that meet perfectly at the back of her neck. She's allowed her wrap to fall a little, revealing a red, skintight shirt. When she smiles at me, the beauty of her homeland beckons. I sit on the ground with the pillows, as she does.

"My name is Samantha." She pronounces it differently. There's a juvenile tingle in my pants and a tightening in my throat I know but have long forgotten. I feel like a schoolboy. But this woman is no teenager. I tell her my name. She gives me a cup of tea as though it were a handshake. "It's a chocolate tea I like. No caffeine. I hope that's OK."

"It's fine," I say, putting my cup down on the small wooden table that separates us. It's too warm. The wood. It feels like its alive. "I actually don't have a lot of time for tea, if you can forgive me for saying so. Someone is waiting for me."

"Tell me what you need," Samantha says, totally unhurried by my impatience.

"I need to speak with Nordeen in confidence."

"You must never be confident in your conversations with that man," she says, grinding her teeth just a tad.

"Then in privacy." I'm still distracted. This woman is releasing the pheromones of a hoard of adolescent girls. It makes her almost irresistible. I have to know. "You are like me?"

"We are kin of a sort," she says, motioning to my tea. "Please drink. What you desire takes preparation if it's not to be painful. I will be ready by the time we finish this pot of tea."

"I mean no disrespect in this, but I should tell you that I'm notoriously resistant to poisoning." She puts on a face of mock surprise, then moves to sly confidence, putting both her hands behind her and leaning back.

"You reveal more about yourself than you do about my character in your assertion, healer. I bid you welcome in my home, Taggert. I will offer you no harm nor will I tolerate it while you stay with me. A man of your . . . skills would no doubt notice the attention you drew coming to this house. These are all my protectors and my wards. If you had any intention of harming me, you would not have made it to my door. The same holds true for any who would try to hurt you now. You are under my protection." She pauses for a minute then continues. "Although if I were truly committed to that ideal, I would not put you in touch with your master."

"I would appreciate it if you didn't call him that," I say, taking big gulps of the tea. It is good. And not poison. "I like to think of him more as my patriarch."

"But patriarchs take care of their children. I mean no disrespect. I only speak the truth."

"But do all truths need to be told?" I'm keeping my voice calm and focused, but she picks up on my frustration some other way.

"You have my apologies. I mean no disrespect to you. I've had no dealing with your . . . employer since the last time we saw each other. Then last night I received a note under my door, similar to yours, telling me that he was calling in his marker. It requested that I stay home until 'a friend from the past' came for a visit."

"You were indebted to Nordeen?" Most who are don't admit it. And I've never met a person who had gotten out from under him.

"A folly of youth. I did not know what he truly was. Even now I don't fully understand what he is. As you are kin, perhaps he is our molesting rich addict of a distant elder. But yes, I owed him. I stayed home today either to kill his emissary or to be killed myself. But the archetypal manipulator chose his only agent who never caused me harm, and who shepherded me from his control to that of my new master." She says *master* like it means father.

I don't know what to say, so I stay quiet and pour more tea, first for her and then for myself. She bows politely like I just impressed her. I'm still trying to figure out if she's flooding my senses intentionally or if it's just natural for her, the way Tamara picks up thoughts. Tamara. The reminder sends my eyes racing for a clock. When I don't find one, it's all I can do to stay seated.

"Will you tell me about the work you're doing now?" she asks as if we're old friends.

"I'm afraid I can't. It's difficult to articulate, and as I said earlier I am in a bit of a hurry." She's looking at me as though I were an idiot but not bothering to explain why. Manners are hard to maintain when the weight of the world is on your shoulders. That's also when they're the most important.

"Your employer didn't explain how this works, did he?" she says with a smile that has little joy in it.

"No. Is it necessary for you to know the details of my business to put me in contact with him?"

"No. But soon I will know enough of your intimate details that these questions will seem trivial. I am ready when you are, Taggert."

I stand quickly and help her to her feet. She smooths her white sarong and guides me by the hand up a flight of stairs. Behind her, the music and the lights fade gently, as though they were there only for her benefit. She leads me to a bedroom where a Japanese glass bed covered in black sheets rests. Nothing else in the room is made of the see-through material. And though there is no carpet and no heating, the room feels as warm as the wooden table downstairs. I barely have time to take everything in before I'm standing in front of a naked Samantha.

Her robe's at her feet. The frail small figure before me looks like a joke of a woman's body. That's what my eyes tell me. That her breasts are small, her hips way too narrow. She barely has an ass. But with nothing between her pheromone-secreting skin and my heightened senses, it's all I can do to keep my hands off of her. Instead, I cough.

"Do you know what my name means?" she asks as though she were not standing naked in front of me. Slowly the lights dim. I look to the wall and see no light switch.

"The feminine version of Samuel, no?" I'm shaking.

"I'm impressed, healer." She does the smile and goes to the black sheets that bind her glass bed tight. "The etymology of Samuel is tricky. Some believe it simply means Son of God. Others believe it means Listener to God. Shem is the tricky part, you see. But it does not matter in biblical terms—for Samuel, the seal of the old judges, was both a seer, a listener of God, and a prophet, a son or gifted one. And as he was, so am I." Mercifully, she gets under the sheets.

"Is it okay to be totally confused now?"

"Yes," she laughs gently. "And thank you for your honesty. Now pay attention. To commune with the man whose name I swore I'd never say in this bed again, you must first commune with me. Your seed must spill inside me. When that happens, I can connect you."

"You are fucking with me." Counterintuitively, I sit.

"Not yet I'm not." She snakes out from under the covers. Her little ass is tighter and rounder than Eve's apple. She rests her head on my lap as I use all my might to resist her trick.

"You're telling me I have to have sex with you in order to talk with—?" Samantha reaches up quickly and silences my lips before I say his name. She nods her head slowly, and her face feels too warm against my pants.

"I will say that your level of self-control is impressive, Taggert. Most men who are around me propose marriage within the first five minutes. I am honored that you've shown such restraint, but if you are in such a hurry then there's no need to delay. You needn't worry about STDs. I'm incapable of—"

"That's not the issue," I snap as I stand. Of course, I'm hard pressed to think what the issue is. Maybe it's the visions of all the prostitutes Nordeen has surrounding him. I always assumed they were throwaway norms. But even in his sexing he recruited, I realize now. "This was your function for him, wasn't it? You slept with people he wanted to have secured conversations with."

"Do you plan on judging me?" She can play it off as mellow as she wants, but, her beautitul head resting on her beautiful hand, I know she's angry.

"No. I don't pity you, either. I want to apologize for my impatience. I didn't realize the process was so intimate." She raises herself to my face. Somehow, her breasts don't seem so small pressed against me.

"You are the only one of his followers that ever deigned to apologize to a whore." I take her face, gently but quickly, and hold her eyes to mine.

"You are no whore." Her mouth is impossibly hot. I'm flushed. She kisses me. I swear she kisses me first.

There is a vast expanse of black openness before me. I do not feel my body. My body is my lodestone. Without it I am powerless. I don't want to panic, but I do. Luckily it's a purely mental panic. No hormones to go awry, no nerves to seize and spasm with a cascading lack of coordination. Just the realization that less than a minute ago I was losing control inside of a woman so beautiful her looks alone could kill me . . . and now I'm incorporeal.

"In the time it took you to meet this vessel, I could have flown to London." It's a young stranger, walking with a cane across an old African savannah in a deep red tribal wrap and headband. The expanse is gone, giving way to harsh, untended grains that scrape at my legs, tiny swarming bugs that move in haphazard patterns, and a setting sun that matches the tone of the stranger walking toward me.

I know the voice and the eyes. Yellow eyes, and the same spittle-infected tone. Nordeen. This is an ancient landscape he strides across, in a time before language. What I am experiencing both has happened and is happening right now.

"Only the faults are mine," I say as I bow my head. I look down and find myself dressed in the clothes I wore in high school. A T-shirt and faded jeans. This is not my body. This is an image of my adolescent body from when Mac was the center of my world. Nordeen once told me one that, in the spirit realm, it is our self-image that we present—the image of what we think we are. But this is not me. I can't feel my body.

"The whore's talent takes some getting used to, there's no denying it," he says and I remember Samantha's insinuation that he is our inappropriate uncle. "But she has her uses. Don't trust a word she says, though." I keep my head low. Part of me wants to ask him why. But that's not why I'm here. Part of me wants to believe him fully, but I also know I was being flooded with pheromones right before I got—

"Where are we?"

"An off-ramp between the Akashic records and the astral plane," he says, taking my arm and continuing to walk a circular path. "It doesn't matter. Speak quickly, little healer. We will be able to communicate like this only so long as your postcoital slumber lasts, and I know how that thing inside of you resists rest."

"I need to know if one of us has backing from greater powers."

"Some of us do. The bitch whose body rests next to yours serves a deviant plant god with plans so surreptitious even I don't know its true orientation."

"A specific one of us." I take note of the strength of the hand that won't let me go. Nordeen's lightly bronzed skin oppresses the veins and muscles in his spirit hand. Is this how he used to look?

"Ah, no doubt you ask about the illusionist." He says with that smile. He puts his young yellow eyes upon me. It's not hard to show deference to this new body. In his prime, I would've been no match for him. But he's in his principal physical shape. How come I'm not?

"She is a pretender to a nonexistent throne," he scoffs viciously. "She thinks there is a pantheon of our kind. She believes she deserves a seat at this imaginary table."

"You know her. Alia?"

"Not her name, before this, but her actions, yes. She sent supplications to me once. I ignored them. I figured a lesser player would take out someone as ostentatious as she before her actions would become worthy of my attention. What did she do to evoke such ire in you, healer?"

"She killed a friend of mine. Another one like us," I say slowly. I'm not ready to lie to him. Even though my powers don't work here, his, whatever they may be, might. But even without my powers I can tell he's about to speak when a crowd appears in the horizon. They are dressed like him, coming out of the sun. But they run as though chased. Some have spears made of iron. Others just wood. All of them men. I wish for my powers and feel nothing. Still, out of instinct I extend my hand against them.

"No need. These are only memories of a long-gone time. Tell me more about your plans for this Alia."

I try and ignore the pleas of the dreams who speak in words so close to clicks and grunts that I'm barely able to distinguish them as language. They throw themselves before us, begging Nordeen for help with some endeavor. He steps over them as though they were rocks or fallen trees. There is no way to understand them, but I imagine them calling to him as a god, as a benefactor. They beg him for aid. Somehow, they can see us. The very memory of their language is no doubt long dead; still, they see us.

"She's way too brazen with her skills, as you say. My friend was connected to someone powerful in the normal world. This girl is responsible for taking them both out. I've got a plan to deal with her, but I wanted to make sure it wouldn't interfere with anything else you had going."

"The girl's illusions are realistic enough. But I doubt she'd expose herself with an open killing. She does brazen, not stupid. On the phone you alluded to there being others," young god Nordeen says.

I need to go careful with this one. But it's hard to pay attention. Another vision from the horizon comes as we walk in a winding down circle. A man, or at least a part man with a lion head, walks toward us. He growls, and I feel it in my body, in my sleeping body. Even Nordeen mumbles something about forgetting how loud the lion man is. He is naked. The supplicants raise their pitiful weapons against him, and already I know they are dead.

"She works with two others. A boy, responsible for the killing. He makes things explode with his mind. And a girl who controls animals."

"Really?" The possessive smile of a kid in a toyshop, one who's finally found his favorite item, takes over the man's face. "And you've seen this animal girl?"

"Yes," I say, thankful I've given him something of interest other than Tamara. "She's Alia's bitch from what I understand. There's no spine in her."

Before I can go on, Nordeen stops our walk to watch the lion man take apart the poor plainsmen who appealed to him for help. One man is bitten and shaken to death by the lion man; the paw-like hands of the creature maul three others. When it's done, the creature growls again in full fury. It's then that Nordeen's spirit body shakes. "This will only take a second," he tells me.

From out of his form, a duplicate pulls itself. I hold on to the man I was walking with as he shakes. When the duplicate fully emerges from the old vessel, I find myself supporting the body of the Nordeen I know, the older man of gray features and tremendous ambiguous power. Yet he still stands erect and angry. The younger body walks in front of the lion man and whispers in the same language as his deceased petitioners. The lion man raises his paw only to be held in check by some unseen power. The younger Nordeen's whispering becomes louder, more inconstant, less like speech and more like idiot-savant scatting. In under a minute the lion man is reduced to a small shell of a lion cub, whimpering and crying as though it hadn't eaten in months. With a quick thrust of the heel, the younger Nordeen smashes the cub's head. He doesn't look back, just keeps on walking. But halfway to the horizon he growls, and his growl has the same sound as the lion man's, only with the spit-infected rattle of Nordeen.

"What the fuck was that?" I'm asking as I stare into the prideful face of the old man.

"A rewriting of history or at least memory" is the closest he'll give me to an answer. I don't push it. "This animal girl. I want her. Deal with the illusionist and her exploding boy as you see fit, but I have uses for a totem controller."

"I can't guarantee—"

"Do you forget your oath?" I look down, and the razor around my neck is hot. Shit, even in my imagination body, I carry it.

"I was only going to say I can't guarantee to deliver her unharmed." It's a lie. A bald-faced lie. And he doesn't catch it.

"Harmed is fine, so long as she still has access to her powers. . . ." He pauses and looks down. Drops of blood paint the ground. I look around quickly, thinking the lion man or the spearmen might have attacked us. But no. The blood is coming from my hands.

"Healer, why is there blood on your hands?"

I'm awake.

The bed is empty when I rise. I dress quickly, afraid that my six-hour time limit is up. I rush down unfamiliar stairs to the scent of chocolate tea. Samantha sits comfortably on a chair, sipping tea and reading a foreign-scripted book. In a brass ashtray lies a joint of something that smells too sweet to be marijuana or hash. She's set a place for me. The same style of ambient music plays as when I first entered the house, but while then it was active and frenetic, it's soothing and passive now.

"You've only been asleep for half an hour. I'd appreciate the chance to speak with you, if your schedule will allow." She doesn't look at me until I speak.

"What is it with you and tea?" I say, taking a seat in the wooden hand chair across from her. I think it's wood, but it feels more like calloused flesh.

"I find it soothes my nerves. Did you get what you need from your employer?"

"You couldn't tell? For some reason I felt like we were inside you, in a bizarre way."

"If I wanted to, yes, I could've listened in. But I have no taste for any business that involves that man." She rinses her mouth with her tea then takes a long drag from her joint. She doesn't offer me any.

"Did you ever?" I venture. "Have a taste for what I do?"

"And what is it that you do, Taggert?" She says it with more pity than I feel comfortable hearing in anyone's voice regarding me. "What does Nordeen use you for?"

"The same thing he used you for, I suspect. To keep those he doesn't know in line, and to keep those he knows afraid of him."

"And you are comfortable with that role?" She pats my hand. Despite the pheromones, I pull back.

"Like you, I made my deal with him when I was too young to know better. And now it's too late. I do the best I can with what I've got. That's all I can do."

"I can offer you more." For some reason I believe her. "I broke his hold over me, and I can tell I'm not as strong as you."

"I was there when you 'broke' from him. You just exchanged one master for another."

"My new lord is as far from Nordeen as we are from the average man and woman on the street." The smoke dances across her eyes, but she doesn't blink. She just takes it in and lets the milky film of tears well up in her deep brown orbs of grace. "Soon my lord will have a vassal strong enough to challenge the Nordeens of the world; the fence-sitters and the opportunists. The vassal will make way for the new growth. You could be part of it."

"You've been with this new lord since you left Nordeen?" She nods vigorously as I take her hand in mine. "If Nordeen sent me here, don't you think he'd know you'd try to convert me?"

"It doesn't matter." She smiles so wide I'm afraid she'll tear her cheeks. "Once you join, you will have the power of us all behind you. Nordeen will not risk open warfare with my lord."

"You'd be surprised what the old man will risk. Besides, I don't want to trade one master for another. Even one as great as you claim yours is." But that doesn't stop her smile. She puts her joint down and clasps my hands with her free hand.

"You don't understand, Taggert. Listen. What are you?"

"I'm a healer." I say on reflex.

"Exactly. Your trek across the Motherland was legendary. Gods took notice. That was who you were supposed to be. Did you know that it was Nordeen who pushed you towards the Dogon? He used them to make you feel inferior, to make you confused. Then, when you were at your weakest, that's when he picked you up. But even then you were not warped enough to be suitable for his handling. When did Nordeen find use for you?" My mind goes back to the year I didn't use my power until the bar fight, and my first realization of the pain I could inflict with my powers. As though she sees my thoughts, Samantha nods in time. "He can only use that which he has twisted from its original form." She pauses, choosing her words delicately.

"Where you just met him . . . most have to lose the most intimate of control to access that place. Nordeen gets there by sacrificing an innocent. This is who you work for, Taggert. Nordeen is a killer. You are no killer, Taggert. At least not by nature. And your nature is important."

I pull my hands away and stand. "I have to go." I walk to the door. I don't hear her footsteps, I don't see her pass me, but somehow she bars my way before I can grab the knob.

"I mean no offense," she says genuinely.

"I know. I can't do this. Someone is relying on me."

"Humanity is relying on you."

"I don't have time for your religion."

"It is not religion, Taggert. It is the reason we exist. We are the liminal ones. We can be poison or prophylactic to the human race." I stop trying to leave and look at her. She's got tears in her eyes. "A battle is coming. A war of gods in which humans' only roles will be casualties. But those like us, liminal ones, we can change the tide. We can make humanity a factor in the war of the gods. Some of them respect us and will speak to us. We can petition on the behalf of humanity. People like Nordeen only wish to throw in their lot with one god or another. Or even worse, pit them against each other, figuring he'll end up on top. He's a spiritual profiteer making gain from the gifts of others. But you don't have to live as he—"

"Enough!" I shout. "This is so far above my head you might as well be speaking another language. I have enough on my plate right now! I have to save a little girl. I have to deliver another one to Nordeen. I have to kill another one! And don't give me that shit about 'it's not in my nature to kill.' I savaged my own brother into a vegetative state with my own two hands before I had my first wet dream!"

"But you didn't kill him," she says, softly touching my face. "And you didn't use the thing inside of you to do it."

"How do you know?"

"I learned a long time ago to assess the eyes of a killer. That's not what you have. You'll kill if it means saving others. And Nordeen has forced you to kill when you didn't want to. But you are no gratuitous spiller of blood. You are only disconnected. You have no true idea as to your name and your function. You play the role of grunt when in truth you are a surgeon."

"I can't leave Nordeen." She nods. "I've got to finish what I'm here for." Again with the nod. "This is all too much for me. Will you quit it with the nodding and say something?"

"Come back." She holds me tightly. I can feel my body giving in to hers. It's remembering what we did before. How we did it, how much I fought giving in for the final time, and how much she wanted me to. In her scent I remember it all.

"When it's all over." She keeps talking. "If you've failed or if you've won or if you've done something in between. If you're broken or whole. If you believe me insane, or Nordeen just too powerful to ignore, come back to me just one more time. You will be welcomed into this house again, and you will not be harmed." When she's done she lets me go. I don't move.

"If I caused you any pain or if I insulted your beliefs . . . ," I offer.

"You've done more than I thought possible from someone in that man's thrall. You spoke honestly and acted in what you thought was the best interest of the both of us."

"I appreciate what you did for me." Again with the nodding. "I don't mean with Nordeen. I haven't . . . It's been a long time since a woman invited me into her bed." I do believe she's blushing. I leave before I have a chance to confirm it.

Chapter Fourteen

"You left me so that you could go get laid?" Tamara is barking this in the tunnel after hugging me with no consideration for my ribs. It's hard to be mad at her.

"I didn't realize that's what it would take!"

"So some guy gives you a note saying go bang this mystical snatch and you just go without questioning it?"

"You're wasting time." I go into the fridge and find something to cool down the burning I'm feeling inside. Free and clear of Samantha's pheromones, and with two hours in transit to process all that I saw, all that I felt, I'm still feeling this burning inside. My body is healthy. But I think I'm angry. "I need locations."

"Locations of what?" She's down to business, still close to my side, like a puppy.

"Rajesh's family restaurant, and the next spot for the Bender party."

"What's the plan?"

"Go kill the fuck out of both of them." I look at her without a hint of humor. "They're not protected by anyone. No one will miss them when they're gone. Fire and hell won't rain down on your head if I pop them."

"What about your head?" The question is tender and genuine. I'm not ready for it.

"I'll be fine. But look, this is your last Get Out of Jail Free card. You can still go running to the government. Tell them who you are, cook up some Iraqi terrorist story and they'll hide you long enough for me to do the deed and get gone. But if you stay in this . . ."

"I'm staying."

"If you stay, there's going to be blood on your hands. Most likely blood from using your powers. It changes you. I'd never wish that on anyone."

"The bitch killed my parents." She stops me cold. I realize she hasn't eaten the food she bought, hasn't showered in days, has passed out more than slept since her parents died. I've met the psychotic compromise of Tamara, and not the real girl. I wonder if her parents would recognize her. "Rajesh, he scares me. I'd take him, but I won't lie. He scares me. That means he'll have the advantage since we both have to think to use our power. But Alia. I was thinking after you left. I never put it together before. She's weak, scared. And she ordered Rajesh to . . . I want her blood on my conscious."

"It's *conscience.*"

"I know what I said and I know what I meant. I want her blood on my conscious. Every morning I wake up, I want to know that I killed the murderer of my mother and father."

"So long as it's a decision you're making." I have an odd feeling of pride. "But if you're down, we've got to work on your skills."

"Mind your gap," she snaps. "I pushed you out a window."

"And still didn't take me out," I snap back. "You squandered that drop on me because you couldn't finesse the move. If you had pushed fifty paperclips through my brain, you would've used less energy and actually achieved something. Instead, you blew your wad on your opening shot and got a mouthful of toilet water in return because you were too weak to defend yourself.

"We've got one shot at this, Tamara. We can't afford any mistakes. These people are like you, not very skilled but extremely powerful. One wrong move and we're out of the game."

"Then teach me what you can. Please."

I feed her first. Chicken vindaloo with some naan and poppadoms at a no-name curry spot with bad service and the best booth we can find. We don't speak as we eat. It's a chore for her. I'm seeing the depression in her for the first time. Insanely spicy hot food gets no reaction.

We're aboveground. and she's got her back to the door of the curry shack. Any of her enemies could come in, see her first and take a chunk out of the girl's back before she had a chance to respond. I try and point it out to her.

"My hair is usually lighter than this. I dyed it. I'm wearing makeup. I never do that. This is not my style. Before I was in skirts, hippy like. Plus, in case you forgot, I'm psychic. I've got stray thoughts from everyone in here."

"Me included?" I ask. Her brow turns down when she realizes she can't read me. "You're what we call a passive reader. Norms have no defense against you, but our type, we can defend against you if we know you're coming."

"How?"

"Different ways. Hard-core telepaths, the ones that only read thoughts, they'd just offer thought confusion for you like 'What color does the sea sound like at dawn?' Or 'Math as the sense-making tool of the universe minus zeroes.' Shit that's confusing and intriguing at the same time. Hard-core telepaths find you peeking around their heads and get you interested in one of their thought puzzles." I slap my hands together quick in front of her face. "They've trapped you. They can keep your mind in a vise for as long as they've got the energy to." She nods, not wanting to refute me, just wanting to learn. As I am with Nordeen. The thought makes my stomach burn again. I think I'm angry with Nordeen.

"Me, I think of a white sheet. Then I imagine totally pure milk poured on that white sheet. Soon I've got nothing in my mind but . . ."

"A blank screen." She nods her head. "It's like meditation with a purpose."

"Exactly. So don't always rely on what you can do. There's ways around everything. Best to do what you can as a norm, and kick up the power only when necessary."

Tamara takes a few more bites of her food before she speaks again. "I knew you wouldn't let anyone move on me anyway," she says. I smile, then stop myself. I'm about to give her the semi-brush-off talk. The "I can help you but I'm not your friend" lecture. But she gives me a blow to the belly first.

"Tell me about my mother."

"That's not going to help us get done what we need to—"

"It would help me," she says softly. "I'm beginning to forget what her voice sounded like, what she smelled like."

"Rose petals dipped in lemon," I say on instinct. Tamara stares at me as I try to ignore my own commentary.

"My mother never told me much about you, aside from the fact that you were friends."

"Smart woman, your mother."

"You realize I'm a psychic, right?"

"And you realize my white sheet is up, I'm sure." I can feel her trying to pierce through my defenses. With proper training and time she'd be able to, if I didn't try to stop her.

"But surely that says something, right? What don't you want me to know about my mother?"

"Nothing." I put my fork down. "Your mother was . . . a kindness to me when I didn't know what kindness was."

"Where did you meet?"

"This isn't the time."

"Bloody wrong about that, you are. Way I see it, we're about to go into what some might call war, yeah? Well, then, this is the part where I get to figure out who's got my back and why."

"Not a chance you can just take it at face value that I'm here for you?"

"That seem like the move of a smart girl, mate?"

"I was at university."

"Which one?" She seems suspicious of the idea I was ever young, let alone a student.

"George Washington University."

"Where the bloody hell is that?"

"Washington, D.C. The States."

"If you're going to take the piss, come up with something better than George Washington University in Washington, D.C. Why not Timothy Leary Academy in Berkeley, California?" I wait for her to stop mocking me. "Why the bloody hell did you go to university there?"

"I'm an American." Tamara sits back a little and smiles. "My family, my home life . . . My brother was a lot like this Rajesh guy. He had powers and was a bully with them."

"Rapist?" she says, not caring who hears her.

"No. Maybe. Truth be told, I don't know. I . . . stopped him. Stopped him cold. But my family still didn't trust me. Couldn't understand what their boys had become, and why one was so different from the other. I was the good one, I guess. But they still couldn't trust me. We barely spoke between the time I stopped my brother and when I went off to G.W."

I slurp down my mango lassi and start working on the soda when I realize I still haven't answered her question. She pulls gently at the sleeves of her hoodie, containing her impatience the best way she can.

"Because my brother was like me, and older, he taught me a lot about my powers early. I knew I was different before I was even your age. By the time I hit college, I was eager to learn everything I could about the body, how it worked. But I also knew I couldn't have a lot of friends, or close friends anyway."

"Hold on, why's that?" I hear concern for her own well-being in her heartbeat.

"What do you think would happen if the norms of the world caught wind of what we can do? Do you think people like us would be worshipped, helped along, given a bit of a boost? Or do you think we'd get stuck in labs to be poked and prodded at until we die by norms we could take apart with a toothpick? At best, we'd be considered nothing more than freaks." I sip on my soda, hard. When I'm done, the teenager takes the cup from me and sips some herself, nodding slowly. It makes it easier to continue.

"I kept to myself for the most part. Took a lot of anatomy and physiology classes, neurochemistry, that kind of stuff. Learned early on how to be a paramedic. Figured it was a good way to earn money and practice my skills. One night we responded to a typical call, alcohol poisoning on campus. This guy is seizing, I mean the shakes and everything. He's about to convulse so hard that he'll snap his own back, but I'm not seeing him."

"You slipped." Tamara smiles.

"What?"

"Your white screen. I just caught your first image of my mother."

"Watch that now," I snap.

"It wasn't me. I mean not really. It was just so strong in your mind, when you look at me, you're looking for her . . ." She stops speaking, looking away from the image in her mind and at me. "My God, you loved her from the first second you saw her." Tamara states it for what it is, a fact.

"For all the good it did me, yes. I loved her from the second I saw her shivering and scared, with a green beer bottle in her hand, wondering what was happening to her boyfriend. I almost blew my cover. I was looking at her for so long that her boyfriend died."

"What?"

"For like a minute. Alcohol poisoning is no joke. But I got his heart pumping again. She thanked me, everybody at that party did, but that was it. I went my way and she went hers. I'd think about her. What she smelled like, how her fingers curved at an almost forty-five-degree angle, the sound of her pulse. These are the things people who can hear bodies listen for."

"So how did you end up being . . . friends?"

"Smoking." A mock look of disgust. "Yes, your mother smoked in college."

Tamara smiles. I'm thinking it's a moment between us. Then I see it for what it really is, a grimace. We keep acting like the person we're talking about isn't dead. We keep talking around it.

"You just walked up to her one day and said, 'Can I bum a light?'" She's back to the story. My history is her distraction. I let her do it. I know I won't even start grieving until those deviant children are burnt and buried in unholy ground. But who am I to say what grieving should look like?

"Close to it. I felt her pulse walking past my dorm, heard the sound the cilia in her lungs made when they caught nicotine. I paid attention to it all for a week, every night around the same time. I didn't even have to look, just sensing her was enough. But then one night I felt an explosion in her brain. That's the only way to describe it—words don't work so well for what we do sometimes. Anyway, I ran downstairs, outside, but all I saw was her smoking. She saw me, remembered me, we started talking . . ."

"What's with the head exploding thing? I mean what is it?"

"It's what I feel whenever one of us uses their power while I'm 'feeling' them. I didn't know that then. It's not like we even talked about it until—"

"This part I know." She nods. "I can tell it to you, if you'd rather. Only, I get the sense it might be a different version than you remember." It's her kindness that's confusing. She leans in and speaks slowly, as though I'm a child. "It's just that my mother really and truly loved my father."

"Tell me what she told you."

"She said she was in a cabin with a friend from school. She had started fires when she was young, but an old Greek Orthodox priest performed an exorcism on her. It scared her so much she never used her powers again, until the cabin. She said you were cooking something and let the flames get too high. They caught the drapes, and it was a log cabin with a pump, and you couldn't pump the water fast enough. So she had to talk the fire down. Tell it to snuff itself. And that was when she had to tell you what she could do."

"She tell you what I could do?"

"Think she tried once, but I couldn't really get it. Still don't, really."

"She tell you we moved to London together?" Shock. She hits me on my arm. "Yes. Your mother and I were close right up until she met your father."

"How'd you get a visa?"

"I told my dad I wanted to marry your mom." When Tamara's pulse slows back down, I speak again. "He was in military intelligence and had connections."

"Why did she break up with you?"

"It's that obvious?"

"You love her now. You loved her then. I don't think you ever stopped loving her."

"These things we can do . . . we can drown in them. I did. All I wanted was to push myself, to see what I could heal, how much, how often, how much food and rest I'd need in order to perform what acts. I regrew a man's arm muscles from almost nothing once. I slept for three days after. At the time, powers were all I cared about. But your mother was trying to get away from them. She wanted a normal life. Your father, he gave that to her. He loved her in a way I never could."

"Where did you go after my mum put you out?"

"Story for another fucking time, kid. Let's get a move on."

We get back to the tunnel after she makes a phone call. The next Bender party is two days away. At the squat, I tell Tamara to pack her things. It's only after she's done she asks why.

"Two days from now, you and I may be dead. I'm not spending my last days in an abandoned tube station." She nods in agreement, and we face the rain of London. It actually doesn't matter to me where I spend my last days. But I can't go into combat with someone unskilled and depressed. I've never had this kind of scrap with one of our kind, only heard about them. You ever hear about a whole town losing its memory, ships at sea that witness water doing things it shouldn't, like talking, or ever just notice a large plot of land that never changes even though the entire neighborhood around it does? That's my kind fighting in one form or another. Croatoan? That was us. My kind don't fight often, because when we do, things get messy for everyone. We generally draw too much attraction to ourselves. An older liminal person (I like the name Samantha gave us), or even one my age, would know this—and we'd find a covert way to handle our differences. These young ones blow up cars in public and attack with a neighborhood full of pets.

We're blunt instruments. Even one reckless blow from a hammer can cripple. So the child—no, I have to call her Tamara, she's no one's child anymore—Tamara is going to have to get good quick. And while anger's not the best cure for depression, it will do in a pinch. Still, her smile emerging from the tunnel for the last time . . . I may die in a couple of days, but I'll carry that smile with me.

I don't let her sleep until we're properly installed in a new hotel, the Abbey Court in Notting Hill. It's high-class for me, but I forget I'm carting a politician's daughter in tow. Tamara shows an adequate amount of appreciation for a room of her own, aboveground, and giggles a little when I offer her the key card.

"And where will you be?" I suddenly remember she's only fourteen.

"I'm next door. Don't worry, I can feel if anything happens to you. I'll be there."

"Promise?" She genuine. She believes the promise to be a legally binding contract. I nod. No smile. I treat it serious. She only hesitates for a second more before disappearing into her room.

The shower feels like warm libations from Samantha's loopy god down my back. I want to sleep in the shower. I've lost faith in my lack of a plan. With no backup from on high, it would seem that the simplest course of action would be to find Rajesh and liquefy his organs one by one until he tells me where his queen bee is. Then I get to kill him and . . . I don't know what comes next. I've been so focused on killing Rajesh. But it will come together once we know what he does. That's my hope, anyway, but I've never taken on three of us at once. Is this a mistake so grand that I'm just too small to see the flaws in my plan? Am I trying to take down a giant by breaking its toes? And what the fuck was up with the lion man?

I dry off and go over everything that happened at Samantha's house. Despite all the bells and whistles and sex, I was able to lie to Nordeen. I can't take it to mean too much. We were on foreign terrain, and he was clearly not himself, but still I lied to him. Plus, he warned me against listening to Samantha, which is a ringing endorsement if I ever heard one.

Unless it's all part of his game. Maybe he wants me with Samantha and her people; maybe he still has a drop on me that I don't know about. I could be the Nordeen infection and not even know it. That's how devious the man is.

A knock on the door, and I scan the person on instinct. It's Tamara. Her tear ducts are overactive. I race to the door in my towel and throw it open.

"I can't sleep. Can you put me to sleep? Like with your power?" I let her in and change in the bathroom. I'm about to use my power, but she's already on my bed, only half awake. I sit on the side and pet her head like I used to do with her mother when finals were killing her. Just like her mom, she mumbles as she falls to sleep.

"I know you lied," she says, barely audible.

"About what?"

"No pain. Mommy was in pain." I breathe in short and nod although she can't see it. "I saw it all in your head. Thank you for lying to me." She goes to sleep with those words.

The carpet is soft enough for me to sleep on. I don't bother with pillows. Some basic part of me doesn't feel like I deserve them.

"You can't think about what you want to have happen," I bark at Tamara. We're in Trafalgar Square, and it's lesson time. "You have to experience it before you see it, before you have any actual physical proof of it happening."

"Like imagination?" she asks, huffing to keep up. I bought her clothes. A thick white hooded sweatshirt and a pair of loose fitting black jeans make her androgynous and ambiguous in this public setting. She's still technically considered missing by the government. Last thing I need is MI5 on my ass.

"No," I snap as I continue to walk, navigating around tourists. "Your imagination exists entirely in your mind. You play about in your head and expect the results of that play in your head. But you should never expect to see what you imagine in the real world."

"You're saying when I turn it on, I should expect results before I see them?"

"Exactly. If you don't, everyone will play you for a novice."

"But suppose I screw up? I've done it before. I thought I'd pick up a table and end up picking up the floorboards."

"You didn't screw up then, did you? Your act had real-world implications. You just lacked focus. Rather than putting your energy into the chair and then deciding to lift it, you focused on lifting, and when you were about to actualize, you pointed at the direction of the chair. Floorboards included."

"OK, got it, all good. But can you tell me why we're walking around in circles?"

I turn on her fast. "This is no meditation. You've got twenty-four hours to learn the basics of what it's taken me years to figure out. And the first thing I learned was that you've always got to think on your feet. Do you understand me? They'll always be norms around. Norms, noise, and distractions. Learn to use your power with all of it going on around you, and you've got the beginnings of skill. But if you're waiting for the quiet room where you can close your eyes and focus, you'll be dead before you matter. Get it?"

She gives the quick nod. I feel like I just took away her favorite doll—the one named Sanity. But there's no time to be subtle. I take the lead, and this time she stays at my right.

"OK, across the square I want you to find a pebble, finger-sized or smaller. I want you to levitate it at eye level and bring it to me."

"People will see."

"Not if you cloud their perceptions at the same time."

"But this place is packed." She's almost whining. "I'll get an aneurysm trying to touch this many minds at once."

"You wouldn't get an aneurysm. I wouldn't let you. And if you're thinking 'everyone' is too hard, then why not just the people in direct proximity to the pebble?" What passes for a smile in a recently orphaned teenager crosses her face. It fades when she tries to sit down. "No sitting. We're walking and talking while we do this."

It takes a good half hour of effort before she's able to do it. Fifteen minutes into it I had to help. But not with the powers.

"You taking a dump in your new clothes or something?"

"Would you please shut up?" she growls, both with her voice and in my mind. She is powerful. A little more force and it would've been a command I'd feel compelled to follow.

"Distractions are part of the game. And stop acting like this hurts."

"It's hard."

"Yeah, but it doesn't hurt. It's on the edge of pain. It's uncomfortable. But you're fine. Breathe. You're not lifting any weight with your body, so relax your abdominal muscles. Get your heart rate to slow down. Relax into this. It's what your mind does naturally." She's stubborn, so it takes her another five minutes to actually take my advice. But when she does, the pebble comes whizzing past my head.

"I did it!" Tourists look confused as she tries to high-five me.

"I said bring it to me, not try and kill me with it. Precision. It's going to be the name of the game."

"But I got it across the square and no one noticed it."

"Child, if you were stripped naked and put in the middle of this square, you'd black out everyone's memory of it before I could say 'Boo.'"

"But that would be different."

"The only difference is motivation. You're not more powerful when you're scared and nervous, just more motivated. Do it again, and remember why we're here. Remember what we're up against. You figured out that flying the pebble across the square was easier on the telepathy side, good. But I still need you to get the telekinetics tight enough to drop the pebble in my hand. Understand?" I guess it's her turn to walk ahead of me.

A minute later the pebble is levitating right in front of my hand. I snatch it out of the air and still feel her power tugging at it until I speak. "Good job."

I make the next exercise harder. I cross the square and put a red X on a pebble. She's got to use the eyes of people in the crowd to find it, then levitate it and send it to me. All without anyone noticing. Doesn't take her long before she finds me hiding by the fountain. I'd changed my face. It didn't delay her. She's better at fourteen than most. Since I know she can read my thoughts, I send out a loud broadcast telling her its break time. She looks a little high when she comes to sit next to me. I hand her a soda. "You didn't mention Prentis," Tamara says after killing the can.

"When?"

"Talking about our plans. You said you'd take care of Rajesh and that I could deal with Alia, but you didn't say anything about Prentis."

"What do you want to do about her?" The girl paces, not unlike her mother, rubbing the palms of her hands together as though she were trying to start a fire.

"I want to let her go."

"Why?"

"No offense, Taggert, but I don't think a man like you will understand."

"Try me."

"She's a victim, yeah? I mean the animal thing is cute and all, but she's got nothing major like I do, or like that viral cunt Alia. And her whole life, she's just been used all the time. Even before the powers. She's more of a pet to everyone than anything else. I mean Alia tells her to jump, and she does. You can tell it's only because she needs the protection. I know what's she's done, what she's responsible for. But God forgive me, I still pity the girl."

"And I wouldn't understand that because . . ."

"Ah, look at you. International traveler, yeah? Mr. Important Man, you are. Plus, you've got the handle not only on your powers but others' as well. You've got that shadow boss and all, but I bet he leaves you alone for the most part. Bet you don't jump through hoops for no one." The razor around my neck gets heavier with each passing word. I'm flushed in the face and will have to work on building up the back enamel in my teeth when I'm done grinding down on them, hard. She speaks of Prentis, and I think of myself. When this girl speaks about me . . . I am not the man she thinks she sees.

"My boss wants her. Prentis. She's the price I pay for being here." How many times can I shock a fourteen-year-old in one day?

"What . . . what will he do to her?" I look away. Fuck if I know. It won't be pretty at first. Samantha's right. He does have to twist people before he can properly use them. Shit, I bet Fou-Fou could talk before he ran into Nordeen.

"Is that what you want to be focusing on?"

"Does he know about me?" the girl asks, shoving me.

"No."

"Well, why didn't you tell him?"

"I promised your mother—"

"Don't be daft, Taggert. You give your boss Prentis, you might as well give him me as well. He'll make her talk. Whatever bullshit story you told him to cover me up will be exposed once he gets her talking."

"I didn't say I'd deliver her articulate." The temperature between us gets subzero. "I can give her a stroke that only affects the language portion of her brain. Tell Nordeen she resisted and that's why. She'll be his. He'll have access to her powers but she'll never speak again. I'll let her know if she ever communicates anything about you, I'll take all her higher brain functioning away."

"Get the fuck away from me." She says it slowly, like she means it. I want to fight, and then realize I'm being compelled. The words echo in the back of my skull as I get some distance from her. I could change my brain chemistry to counter the effect, but she's right about needing space from me. I'm the monster in the box, a better weapon than Prentis for a more ruthless swindler than this Alia girl. I know it. Tamara just learned it.

There's a nice pub right behind the bus station. I take up residence in a booth and take down three ciders before Tamara comes to find me. I use them for the sugar. She orders one for herself. She's way too short and young looking for the bartender to serve her, but she's got the passive use of her powers in check.

"I shouldn't have judged you." The drink is for me. Same cider I was drinking. She was in my mind as well.

"Yes, you should. Just because it's harsh, doesn't mean it's not valid. I've done barbaric things. . . ."

"Because you've had no choice." It's more a question than a statement.

"We always have choices, don't we? I chose, choose to serve a man who could teach me about my powers."

"The way you've been teaching me?"

"Yes, only instead of using pebbles, he had me use people. People like us. Someone described us as liminal people. You know what that word means? Always on the borderlands, the threshold, the in between. I learned what I know by walking the liminal lands, Tamara. That work changes a person. Even someone who couldn't change his face, his weight, his body the way I could. I chose to walk that land, to do that work. It is mercurial, confusing labor with no standards or norms, Tamara. Notions of good and bad are irrelevant when dealing with people that can turn a continent into a wasteland or a soul into a compost heap. Some of those people I had to treat like allies, others I buried so far beneath the ground the worms are still looking for them. And in the end, I don't know what savagery I did because of where I was, and what madness I concocted because I was told to by a man . . ." Anger wells in my throat. Unconscious reaction to the vision of Nordeen in my mind. Why can't he just go away?

"I don't even know what his powers are." I breathe in harshly and put my head back in the booth for a second. I'm lucky that I open my eyes just in time to see Tamara reaching for the razor around my neck. I grab her hand tightly with mine.

"It's your leash, isn't it?" she says softly, flinching at the word *leash* but unable to find a better substitute. I nod. "I didn't realize before. You aren't always like this."

"Like what?"

"Confident, so assured. You're a slave." She knows there is no better word for what I am. I nod again. "You're on leave. Loaned out . . ."

"And when I go back . . ."

"Why in the name of all that's good would you want to go back?"

"*Want* is a word that left my vocabulary a good seven years ago. What I need is to not have that man pissed off at me. I need for you to be safe and totally ignorant as to the depravity that Nordeen can inflict."

She takes a sip of cider before she speaks. "You risked your world, as demented as it is, for a chance to see my mother again?"

"Things were simpler for me, for us, when I was with your mother. I missed those times."

"You really loved her." I nod. "Why do you think she broke up with you?"

"Because I'm too much of a fixated moron to know when the only woman I'd ever truly love in my life was slipping through my fingers. I was more focused on mastering these skills than on making her happy. She called me a freak. In a letter. Told me she was leaving and that I was to be gone when she got back."

"I know she left you. But somehow, I always got the sense you left her first."

"Maybe I did, in my own way. But that was years ago, and memory has a way of telling you the things you want to hear. . . ." A possibility hit me. I do the math. I look at the girl sitting in front of me. White milk on white sheet.

"What?"

"Nothing. It's time."

"You just shut me out. And time for what?" She's complaining as I'm standing and getting ready to go.

"Dangerous place for you to be," I say, tapping my head. "It's time for the Indian. You ready?"

"Sure. Where to?"

"You tell me. Where'd you say his parent's restaurant was?"

The cabbie lets us out in White Chapel in the rain, across a busy street from the restaurant. There's a bench that offers a view of the red stone library and not much else. We take it. The Indian restaurant is not much more than a small step above a curry shop. From the front, it looks like a small store shop, but when I read the consistent strain of a heavyset Pakistani man's legs, I understand how deep the place is. I use the same man's eyes to survey the restaurant, a process not unlike looking through a telescope with sunglasses on. I want to control his body, tell his neck muscles where to turn his head, but I can't control his mind and I don't want panic to set in . . . .. not yet. I'm about to ask Tamara to scan for me when I realize that the rain isn't hitting either one of us, and an explosion is occurring in her brain.

"He's not in there." Tamara says. I recognize the courage it takes for her to try and touch minds with the rapist that killed her parents.

"Remember, he's mine. I just need you to point him out."

"He's tough."

"I dissolve tough like acid."

"What happens if he's traveling with Alia and Prentis?"

"Dog girl will scare away easy enough. As soon as she uses her powers, I'm killing every animal she brings. With illusionists, the trick is to get them to see something that isn't there."

"I don't get it."

"Don't worry about it. If this Alia is as big a party organizer as you say, I doubt she'll be spending the night before a major festivity slumming with her muscle."

We stay still. Waiting. Even when the typical London drizzle turns to downpour, we don't move. Tamara just gets up under me. At first I think she's looking for shelter. But the closer she gets, the less rain beats down on my head. She uses her telekinetics to keep us relatively dry. I want to chastise her for doing it, afraid it might draw attention, but this whole project is hard enough, and her attention never slips from the door. An hour and a half later, a broad-shouldered man roars his Japanese-made motorcycle off the road and onto the busy sidewalk. Mothers of small children grab their sons and daughters then chastise the biker.

Rajesh takes off his helmet. His short-cropped hair is oiled and pushed back. His big-boned face uses his eyes as a threat. "Try me," they say. No one does. He strides into the restaurant, not even bothering to lock his bike up.

"That's him." Like she had to tell me.

"Stay here," I tell Tamara without looking at her. "I've dealt with his kind before. I've got this. You'll just get in my way. About ten minutes after I go in, customers will start running out. When you're sure it's just me and him in there, lock the doors with your power. All of them, front, back. Shit, do the windows just for good measure. Lock the place up tight." I feel her whole body shudder and know it's not the rain. It's the sight of the arrogant prick that likes to blow people up from a distance.

I keep my features static as I walk into the restaurant and ask for a table in the back of the shotgun-style eatery. I can see everyone. He's not in here. From my table I can see the steps in the kitchen leading up to an apartment above. When they offer food, I decline.

"You should probably leave now," I tell the old man, the rapist's father. His belly is too big for his shirt, let alone his pants. But it's corpulence born of midlife indulgence after juvenile poverty.

"I am sorry but I don't—"

"I'm here for that walking corpse you call a son." I sense the malnutrition the old man grew up with and know he's an immigrant and not a native. His swollen belly symbolizes his success, not excess. I don't know what he sees in my eyes, but it's enough to make him to try and carry his wife out quickly. She resists, and when she demands to know the cause of the fuss, he whispers in her ear. Then he points to me. She gathers the excess cloth of her sari in her right hand and shimmies her pigeon-toed frame to my table.

"He is my son," she says with a passion I'm hard-pressed to find a place for. Long ago, someone told the dark Indian woman that once she got married she would never have to worry about anything again. Then I showed up in her life. She tries again when I sip my water. "He is my only child."

"Do you know what he does to other people's children?" I ask, sipping my water. She does. I can feel the clench in her jaw, the knot that is always there and just won't go away. If she's not careful she'll develop lockjaw, or grind her teeth to dust.

"He can change." The only compassion I can offer is stifling my laugh. I finally look in her round, pudgy face. It melts in shame before me. To the old man's credit, he grabs his wife's arm before he walks out of the restaurant without a sound. They could be going for the police. That'd be bad for the police.

I send the cooks out of the cramped kitchen with massive cases of tinnitus that stop as soon as they leave their illegal work hole. Those who manage fire and spices are superstitious by nature, so a bad ringing in the ears while they ply their craft—as well as a missing owner and his wife—is enough to cause a labor strike Trotskyites would be proud of. Now the patrons are confused, and a little scared. I give them enough dopamine to keep them calm and seated. I'm waiting for my moment. Finally, Rajesh descends the stairs, alerted by the commotion. His body speaks volumes before his lips even move. His bones are hypercompacted, near reconstructed. That only happens from repeated breaking or countless fights . . . or both. Muscles strangle each section of Rajesh's skeleton, apparently demanding any smidgen of fat they can find. I know I can't see any. His body, like his constantly exploding mind, has been shaped by fulmination. He walks right by me; my table is obviously used for those who want a little privacy. Major mistake to give me a chance to hide in the shadows.

I time it perfectly. I generate nausea in every person he passes. They vomit when in close proximity to him. I make everyone allergic to his smell. They run from the restaurant, appalled by him. The parents' reputations will never survive. They shouldn't have had a rapist kid. He's confused now. Angry. And . . . Yes. The increased adrenaline, the lowered serotonin. Now he's frightened. Only now will I speak to him.

"I'd blame the pakora." I smile as I stand. He's by the doors, pulling against them and realizing that he can't get out.

"Who the hell are you?" There's no hint of Indian accent in him. He's all East End thug, listening to way too much hip-hop.

"Come on, Rajesh. You try and kill a man, you should at least remember his face." I start walking toward him.

"You're going to have to narrow that down a little, mate. I've killed a lot of people." He doesn't get it. He thinks we're going to fight. With our fists. Moron.

"Yeah, from a distance. Isn't that how your faggot power works? Never have to move in and do the damage personally?"

"So it's powers we're talking about now, eh?" He stops walking for a second to concentrate. He explodes the table to my right into so much kindling. "That's mine. What's yours? Aside from making people throw up, I mean?"

"I kick punk rapists' asses for a living. And your little boom-boom show don't mean shit to me." He's stopped moving. He's trying to use his powers. I counted before. Three-second delay from when he stopped walking to when the table exploded. Tingle in my chest. He wants to explode my heart. I grab a bowl off another table and tag him in the head.

"Eyes open, Rajesh. I want you to see this ass kicking coming." He wipes the spicy curry off his head and is about to charge me when he stops of his own accord.

"Wait. I recognize you now. You're the bloke in the limo, with that little skank's parents. I didn't know you were one of us."

I'm trying hard to let the "us" part go so I can gain information. It's the only reason he's still alive, after that bullshit attempt at blowing my heart out of chest cavity. "If you weren't after me, then why blow the car?"

"Talk to Alia," Rajesh says with a more casual demeanor. He thinks he's got nothing to worry about. "She said taking out the parents would leave the girl no place else to go. Is that her, holding the doors tight?"

"You geniuses ever think about the repercussions of getting someone like 'us' really mad at you?"

"Yet to meet a fucker I can't make jam out of, you included, geezer. No offense, old timer."

"You are an offense," I say loudly. "Plus you're thicker than a post. You're two seconds from dead, asking, 'Are we there yet?'"

"Look, you want the one who gave the order to blow you up, go talk to Alia. If you can find her. You want to scrap one-on-one, stop bitching and bring it. I'm tired of your mouth, grandpa."

"You killed the only woman I ever loved. Die now." He throws a chair at me before I can get the seizure I wanted started. Seizures are too complicated. I should've just clenched all his muscles. Too late. He's on me.

He's borrowed a page from my book, trying to keep me from concentrating. I'm up against a wall, and he's ramming his shoulder into my ribs. But now I've got his head. I go nuts, grow bone spikes out of his collarbone. If they're painful, he doesn't show it. He just tosses me halfway across the restaurant. I land hard, but he's still a little discombobulated. He's got two powers, like Tamara. He can make things explode, and he's superhumanly strong. Knew there'd be a catch.

Rajesh explodes the air in front of me. It doesn't hurt, just a distraction. I catch the stool he throws but miss his charging into my sternum again. This time he's smart. He doesn't stay with me. Just knocks me back to where I was sitting before. Luckily, I'm still holding the stool, because when he starts exploding the restaurant stereo equipment around me I need something to brush it all away with. He thinks I don't see him circling behind me. I dehydrate him almost completely so he knows who he's dealing with.

Doesn't stop him from ramming me in the back again, though. He's like a damn bull. He didn't drink any water; there's just more to him than I thought. I slowed him down but didn't dehydrate him fully. He thinks he's slick. It's punches now, only each one is prefaced with an air explosion. I can take them. I can take them all day. He doesn't realize it. He's never boxed; he doesn't know how to take a punch, how to bring a sucker in, get him worn out from throwing his own punches then make him wish his momma never squeezed him out.

I take everything the young buck has to offer. He explodes bones, organs, air, limbs, every piece of me he can. He uses those hands like tenderizers and tries to make mincemeat out of my face, my chest, my groin, my ribs, and my back. I give him just enough resistance to keep him going. What damage he does, I heal swiftly. After all, I am a healer. We wreck the restaurant entirely before moving it to the kitchen. He tries to shove my face into hot oil. That I can't allow. I duck under and tip him so his hand goes in instead. He screams in a tongue he hasn't spoken in since childhood. That's some serious deep-fried pain. A pain so big he can't concentrate. No concentration equals no powers. He's mine.

I make his flesh like putty, reach into his chest and grab his ribs with my hands. All of a sudden the pain of a crispy-fried hand is nothing. I keep his pain receptors wide open as I lift the big boy over my head. Just as his ribs break, I throw him back into the restaurant proper. He can barely move. I'm tired of physical combat. I calcify his skin, shrivel his testicles to the size of raisins, evacuate his bladder and intestines and start a slow buildup of fluid in his lungs.

"Alia . . . ," he manages to get out.

"What about her?"

"It wasn't my fault. It was Alia." He's spitting up something green and black.

"We all make choices in our lives though, don't we, buddy?"

"I can help you. I'll tell you everything you need to know about her."

"Will she be at the Bender party in Soho tomorrow night?" Fucker actually tries to stall. I break three of his vertebrae and make his bone marrow allergic to his blood type. "Will-she-be-at-the-Bender-party-tomorrow-night?"

"Yes, oh God, Yes!"

"Then what the fuck do I need you for?"

"You can't see her. You don't know what she looks like!"

"Forgot so soon about the girl whose mother and father you killed? She knows what your lady's face is all about. Again, I don't need you."

"No! She doesn't!" Problem. I'm thinking. "No one does."

"Prentis, the dog girl. She knows." I hate the level of questioning in my voice.

"No, she doesn't! Alia wouldn't trust her to take out the garbage, let alone with her real face. She doesn't trust anyone."

"But she trusts you? You're muscle, not confidant. You're over-playing your hand, 'jeshi."

"No! Don't kill me." I'm not even trying to make him cry. "I wasn't supposed to see. She sleeps alone 'cause she can't maintain the illusion when she's asleep. I had to deliver some money to her one time. I guess she was tired. She was sleeping in her living room. I saw her! I saw her!"

"So you woke her up and she let you live? Bullshit!"

"I snuck out!" he screams. His nerve endings begin to grow out of his fingers. I'm fucking with his insides like a vicar on a whore. "I snuck out. I knew she'd kill me. I snuck out. I knocked on the door hard when I came back. I swear. She looked different then. Like she always does. I swear I saw her."

"So here's a question, boom boy. And take your time answering . . . it's your only reprieve from drowning in your own waste. All this girl does is make illusions. Images you know aren't real. Meanwhile, you blow things up. Plus, she's a woman, and we both know how you really feel about women. So how is it you end up taking orders from this Alia chick?"

"Fuck you, you arrogant prick."

"Ah, see, now you're tasting your own mucus and blood again. Keep it civil and I'll give you a decent death," I lie. "Now answer my question."

"You've never met her." Is that a laugh through the grimace of pain? I have to hold back from sending multiple blood clots to his brain. "It's not images, it's not illusions. When she's got you in her grip, when she holds your brain it's not illusions . . . it's reality. I've seen her put a guy in fire and watched his skin boil. Her imaginary swords draw blood. Fuck, the only way I know you're not her is I just left her. She runs everything around her. She's like her own planet, complete with her own gravity. . . ."

"So why does she want me so bad?" I've been so focused on my torture thing that I didn't feel Tamara come in. Her steps are delayed, like she's approaching a wounded animal. I want to reach out to her, tell her there's nothing to worry about. That I've got her. But she gets stronger with each step, and I realize it's not my place.

"Why? Why all this killing and intimidation? What makes me so special?"

I can tell he wants to say something dirty and nasty. But his bloodshot eyes look at mine and see what I want. He speaks plainly.

"She thinks that with you, she'd actually be able to do all the things she makes people think. She calls you her retarded sister. . . ." Tamara spits at the idea. "She says you were meant to work together. That's why she was so angry when you turned her down. She took it personal. I'm nothing to her. Prentis, less than nothing. But you . . . your parents were in the way. That's all. The way she said it, she said it like no one would notice. No one would care."

"I care." She's trembling with rage. Everything around us begins to tremble as well. Her telekinesis is fusing with her emotional state. I almost let my focus slip when I imagine the possibilities of that. "What about Prentis?"

"What about her? You've seen Alia with her. She does whatever Alia says. The only time Alia lets her do or say anything is when she wants to make fun of her or put her down."

"And you and Prentis?" I have to ask. He gives me another look, shakes his head vigorously. He knows what's coming. To push him along I twist his calf so tightly it begins to atrophy.

"Oh God! Yes, I did it. Alia gave her to me."

"*Gave* her to you?" Tamara's shaking had stopped for a moment, only to start up again when Rajesh spoke. "How are you *given* another human being?"

"You don't understand! Neither one of you pricks understands. When you're around Alia, she can give you whatever you want. She looks in your mind, and your best desire, or your worst fear, that's what she can offer you. I wanted women, lots of them. I didn't know if she was making me look different, or them look different. Or if I was with anyone at all. It could've all been in my head. The first few times I had Prentis, she made me think that she was her, that Prentis was Alia. I didn't . . . I didn't know."

"He's lying!" Tamara shouts loud enough in his mind to reverberate through his body. "He knew Alia wouldn't sleep with him. He resented that she was trying to pass off Prentis as her, so . . . oh my God, you vulgar fucking creature, you . . . raped her until she bled, and you liked it."

"Get out of here now, Tamara." She looks at me harshly. I can't return it. Hang around Nordeen long enough you'll meet some sport rapists. The type that makes this pool of physical and mental sickness at my feet seem like a romantic. To keep the peace, I've had to sit through more than a few of their glory-day stories as they tried to convince my boss to switch from hash trading to bonded child chattel, to slavery. If he did take it on, Nordeen was smart enough to keep it from me. Maybe he caught wind of my emotions when they spoke. At least I had the filter of words. Tamara just experienced the situation from the rapist's perspective. Even disheveled and powerless, this fucker is toxic.

"I can't have you doing my killings for me." She's trying to use logic as the whole building around us shakes with her rage.

"You're mad right now. You think taking this asshole out will make you feel better. It won't. Only thing that'll make you feel remotely sane again is knowing that what happened to you won't happen to someone else. That's not him, that's the queen bitch, Alia. You take this sap out, you'll be questioning yourself all your tomorrows." Truth is, I can't stop her if she's committed. So I think of offering praise to Samantha's cult god when the building stops shaking. She looks at me, nods, and leaves.

"Please, I helped, yeah? I told you everything, right? Don't be a bastard, come on, help a guy out. I was confused yeah? Didn't know what was going on, for real. I'll change." I can barely understand him through his crying.

"Shh, relax. This isn't going to hurt." I start flooding his brain with heroin levels of dopamine. "I'm going to heal you now." And I do. His entire body. From the hurts I've imposed to every hereditary defect that would've caused even an ounce of pain in his late eighties. I turn him into an ultimate specimen of humanity, of liminal humanity even. He can't believe his luck. Then he sees me smile.

I start again by exploding every one of his taste buds. I burn his liver and intestines with lactic acid, turn his stomach into a Swiss cheese–like membrane and fill it with the remains of his bone marrow. Just before I increase the pressure in his eye sockets until vision becomes unbearable, I dry out his eardrum, making balance an impossible notion. I regrow the bone spikes from his neck, legs, and arms almost as an afterthought. By the time I'm finished with him, he uses his last remaining power to explode his own head.

I walk from the restaurant to the early evening. Across the way, Tamara sits sobbing on the bench where I left her. Fourteen years old. I hadn't done this much at her age. Mac ran the town, really just the high school, but that was it. He held court over all the local teenagers and the poor teachers associated with the school, but there were no global conspiracies, no murder of parents to get what he wanted. And all I did was follow behind him, tending to every bump and scrape that he might have. I wouldn't have been able to handle what this girl is facing.

"It's over," I tell her, petting her hair.

"I want you to know." She moves my hand only so that she can look in my eyes. "I don't think of you as my dog. My killer. I know what my responsibility is. When the time comes, I promise I won't let you down."

"I know."

"I'm not like them. Alia and Rajesh. I'm not hard like them. But I'm no Prentis, either. I can handle myself."

"Better than I could at your age." She nods, realizing there isn't a hint of patronization in my voice. "Right then. Let's get suited up."

Chapter Fifteen

Soho has been taken over by samurai. From Chinatown to Covent Gardens to the West End proper, the spirit of feudal Japan has linked up with drum and bass to cause a pagan-like celebration—something London hasn't seen since the initial explosion of the Jungle scene. All the shops, from the Chinese dumpling palaces to the high-end sex-toy retailers, are participating. Proprietors stand outside their shops asking people to come in for tea. Japan doesn't have this many kimonos.

The boundaries of the outdoor party are marked by eight huge video projectors, apparently linked to some camera in the crowd. I didn't think London could party like this anymore. The music is overwhelming the closer you get to some speakers, but there are some relatively quiet zones as well, where you can have a conversation without shouting. There are very few people in those zones. Five DJ's compete with varying sound systems for the attention of the crowd. They have mine until I feel the orphan next to me tug my jacket.

"How the hell are we going to find her in this?" Tamara took good advantage of the theme. She's painted her face white, with a red dot on each cheek. Nothing on the planet would get her into anything white so soon after her parent's death, and black would make her look too much like the assassin she's planning on being. So we decided on a deep blue kimono, and a real sword just in case this plan goes all types of pear-shaped.

"She'll find me," I say, pointing to the video projectors. I stand out because I'm not wearing a kimono. A few others in the crowd aren't either, but they, too, are marked as different. Either they stumbled into this disorganized co-option of public space, or they've just never been to a Bender party. Apparently there's always a theme involving costuming. Guess it fits the personality of an illusionist. I look down at the girl I've held and talked to and worked with for three days. It seems like months. Even with face paint on, she reminds me of her mother. This may be the last time I see either one of them. "Get lost, before we're spotted together."

I've trained her well. In a second she's under the group miasma of the party. Like the ninja she dressed as when we first met, she disappears into the crowd. What's more, no words. Just action. My turn to do the same.

I find one of the cameramen. He's bouncing his little digital camera on the breasts of a girl not much older than Tamara, and I take it from him. I shine it on my face, then the razor around my neck. Then my face again. I toss it back to him. For almost fifteen seconds my features and my master's calling card were writ large on the big screen. This Alia chick is all about control. I just interrupted the flow of her control for a few seconds. If she's worth her salt, I'll be getting a talking-to any second.

I pull three chicken buns from a local vendor before a big black bruiser taps me on my shoulder. He speaks less with his words than his body, which makes sense as I am in the middle of a roaring crowd bouncing up and down to an old Congo Natty tune. He tells me with his eyes that the lady of the evening wants to have a conversation. One scan and I know him for her Fou-Fou. He'll come for me with the .380 he has under his jacket if he needs to. But his task is only to bring me to his mistress.

I keep one of the buns and follow the bruiser as he pushes through crowds of barely post-teen drunkards and tourists with more money than common sense. He leads me to a flight of stairs between two flats, a stairway that shelters five people. All muscular, like my friend behind me. I could take them down in a second. Instead, I play the part and climb the stairs with an arrogance that causes men who outweigh me by a hundred pounds to rethink any moves they might make.

The steps lead to a huge old flat tarred roof, a rarity in the neighborhood. Thirty people drink, pop pills, and dance on this street-party version of the V.I.P. lounge. Across the street, another roof party. Down the block, another one. It's really the next level up. Right on the edge of this rooftop, an impossible woman reclines on a chaise lounge with a cigarette installed in an old-school two-foot-long filter. The woman is emaciatedly thin, like an anime character with cartoonish ovals for eyes and cheekbones that extend up to her earlobes. She sports a red dress patterned with dragons. Dragon Lady. I know her to be Alia without my big bodyguard offering a directional hand in her vicinity.

I allow myself to be guided but then I catch a familiar body in my sensory periphery. As I veer right, the bodyguard tries to stop me. I turn him into a diabetic in desperate need of insulin. Once I'm free of him, I return his pancreas to working order. His insulin will rebound. Or it won't. Prentis, dressed as a Japanese rice peasant, complete with rice-paddy shoes, torn pants, and blouse, tries to run from me. I give her a leg cramp and continue to walk slowly toward her. It's only when she stands, lip quivering, I realize I don't have much hate for her. She did attack me, she was part of all this, but I'm finding some kinship with her. I'm looking in her face, trying to find the opportunist that I saw in Rajesh, the power hunger I expect from Alia, even the misdirected anger of Tamara when we first met. Instead, all I see is her pure, abject terror. And while I know it's probably Alia's rage she's afraid of, the girl is looking at me. What's more, I know what I'm going to have to do to her later in order to keep Tamara safe. I feel the perversion of my power as I finger her brain. That sense, reinforced by her garb, disgusts me.

"Run away. Run now and never let me see you again." When she obeys, I start screaming in my head, "What about Nordeen?" Another problem, another day.

The Dragon Lady rises briefly from her seat to investigate the commotion, but refocuses on her cigarette as soon as Prentis runs down the stairs. I walk calmly over to her but wait for her to speak.

"I have it on good authority that you killed my man Rajesh," she tells me like she read it in the paper next to the sports column. It's disconcerting talking to a voice you're not sure has been spoken. Even that could be an illusion.

"I didn't come all this way to speak with an illusion," I state with the same disdain. She turns from overlooking the party and finally meets my eyes.

"Well, my dear. If you hadn't have killed one of my soldiers, scared my favorite puppy dog away, and broken one of my norms before even saying hello, you might not have wasted your trip." She says it in a long, drawn-out posh drawl that doesn't match her image.

"Is that the message you want me to convey to Nordeen Maximus?" She turns quickly at my words. I notice the ash she flicks disappears into thin air. It's all illusion. I'm not talking to the girl, but she's somewhere close by. Close enough to hear me and have her illusion respond.

"Anyone can buy a razor," she says snidely.

"Yeah, but no one invokes Nordeen's name without knowing who he is. And you can't know who he is and try to claim him without intimate knowledge."

"Nordeen sent you?" There's a level of hope in her voice. I nod. Suddenly, the landscape changes. I'm still on a roof, but I'm a lot closer to the edge. The Dragon Lady I was talking to disappears, and where she was is only sky and the gentle updraft of Chinese food and body funk. Two more steps. If I tried to touch the Dragon Lady I would've fallen. This Alia girl is good. From behind me another voice, different from the Dragon Lady, continues the conversation. "Then I welcome you as the emissary from one power to another."

I turn to face a woman of my height, with flowing black hair and a white Kimono. She walks on shoes with wooden slots at the soles. Her face is small, Middle Eastern, and intense.

"I didn't think he'd received my gifts," she says, sipping on a glass of champagne.

"They were not to his liking," I reply curtly. Time is running out. She's made me. Now I need to make her for Tamara.

"What else could I have offered his petulant highness that would have appeased him?" There's that put-upon air about her again.

"What you covet the most. I'm here to take the telekinetic back to my lord. He says any further involvement between you and her will result in war between our two camps." She puts the glass down, and I've figured her out again.

"That girl is mine. I found her first, she's in my city—"

"Yes, your city where you ordered a public execution of a highly political norm because you couldn't use your sway to convince the girl to come to your side."

"And you know this how?"

"Your muscle doesn't know how to keep his mouth shut when he's seizing in agony. And as I said earlier, I did not come all this way to speak with an illusion." I turn and hit the stairs. The bodyguards know better than to interfere with my progress.

Some grime jam is making the crowd in this section of the street jerk around like headless chickens. I just keep walking. This is all part of the plan. Alia controls her environment, so I've got to get her out of control. Get her questioning and unsure. Get her to drop her own illusions. Just once. Can't risk using my power on her. If it's not her body, she'll know I tried to get her and she'll attack. If I can't tell what's real and what's not, then I'm no use.

"Wait!" The bark sounds more like a real voice, but it's way too loud over the music. It's indicators like this that are the only way I can tell if she's real or not. The champagne glass on the table didn't make a sound. Now her voice comes through, though I'm nowhere near a quiet zone. Means she's projecting into my mind. Still, like a fish on a line, I've got to draw her in. So I stop and turn.

"You take the girl and I get what in return?" Alia asks.

"The thanks of a power that can break you whenever he so desires." Now she's a blonde, Caucasian, still gorgeous but totally different than the last two images she put up.

"That's strange." She laughs, almost trying to circle me. "Because my understanding was that Nordeen hardly ever left his little hiding spot anymore. I hear he's afraid of London. I hear his power is waning, and if it weren't for his emissaries he'd have no power at all."

"So what are you saying?"

"I'm saying let's sit, have a drink, discuss things." I look to my right, and once again there's something I wasn't expecting. On the sidewalk, fifteen feet in front of me, in one of the more quiet sections of the Samurai Bender, is a small table with two chairs, sake, and a host waiting to seat us. I'm praying Tamara doesn't take her shot as I pour white milk on sheets. No doubt this Alia has some mind-reading skills of her own. I sit in my chair and notice when her chair rocks a little as she sits. Good. There's a body in it. Now the real question is, whose body?

"I think I know who you are," she starts after pouring a cup of sake for herself, drinking, then offering it to me. "You're the old man's healer, no? I haven't met a lot of people like us. Seven, maybe eight. But a disproportionate number of them know about you. You are the cautionary tale for people like us, did you know that?"

"And this is your sales pitch?" I say, genuinely annoyed.

"As you implied earlier, what do I have to sell? Nordeen takes what he wants, just as the norms do as they please with no understanding that their betters walk amongst them every day."

"So why am I drinking sake with you?"

"Because you and I both know it doesn't have to be like this. We are the rightful heirs of this planet. But we are kept in the shadows by manipulative little old men like Nordeen."

"Watch your mouth, woman. You've got no idea of his power."

"Neither do you." She stops me cold. "Neither does anyone else who has had dealings with him. And there are others like him. Old people like us, who use others to get what they need. I've got no problem with that. Why do the heavy lifting when you can get someone else to do it for you? But you've got to be able to prove to the new blood, like myself, that you can still get your hands dirty if necessary."

"And you chose to draw the line in the sand with this girl?" I sneeze. The illusionist doesn't catch it.

"Perhaps. You see, I think Nordeen and I are just about equally matched right now. He has you razor-necks, and a few other powers like yourself. But I've got resources as well. Now, if I were to get Tamara on my side, our battle would no doubt flame the world from here to whatever little hidey-hole in Morocco your man has. But if I were to have *you* on my side as well, I don't know if Nordeen would risk it."

For the past five seconds I haven't been paying attention, but I've been trying to act like I have. It's her. I can feel a body, a circulatory system, respiration, the explosive brain, all of it. And it jumps when she says Nordeen. She knows who it is. The sneeze was the cue. Tamara's a witness, somewhere. I don't know where she is. But she's got to be seeing this. She needs to move now. There's a shift in Alia. She knows I haven't been paying attention. She's putting it together. Where the fuck are you, Tamara?

"Why does a healer sneeze?" It almost feels like an earnest question.

I hear Tamara's voice say "Get down" a second before four darts fly from directly behind my head directly into Alia's brain. At least, where it should be. The darts fly through the head without any effect. She's another illusion. But I know she's in the chair.

159

"Good effort." Alia's way too congratulatory. She's got that Nordeen smile. I stand. "Uh-uh," she chastises. "My turn."

The world is black. The world is white. The Bender party is gone. I am gone. Fuck. Alia has me.

I'm being thrown out my window. I'm a kid again. It's the tree. I'm thrown into the tree through a wall. Fucking Mac. But it's different. This is when I healed myself for the first time. Mac saw me do it. He treated me like a real little brother. For a little bit, he loved me. It's the beginning of the "good days," before I healed my mom, before I learned the difference between good and bad. This is supposed to be a good memory. But it's something different. My brother's teeth are huge, made for devouring. And I can't feel his body.

"You tried to kill me." He's bigger than life, lording over me, his huge teeth aimed at my face. Fuck! It's this girl. This Alia, I know it is. There's no other reality, no other sensory input. Its just Mac coming for me. It's not real. Doesn't matter. I'm running. I'm running. I've failed and I'm running. . . .

I'm in a car. No! Not his car! Yasmine and her husband. No, it's not Yasmine. It's my mother. She's not a vegetable. She's kissing Fish'n'Chips. They're kissing. In love. Please stop this, you stupid bitch.

Her power is sloppy. I am feeling this all, seeing it, experiencing it, but it's not a coordinated experience. This is the flickering reality of an ADD-addled sociopathic illusionist. No! Explosion. It's a blood-rain parade. I've got her arm in my hands . . . Whose arm? Yasmine or my mother? They re-form. I can feel the severed nerve endings looking for their frayed partners. Charred skins sloughing off their blackened pieces to form layers of red and white tissue. Wrapping torn and burned muscle tight. It's forming a body. It's a disgusting amalgam of flesh and bone that has no distinct parts, no head, or chest, or eyes. This is what I felt the first time I hurt someone with my power. And it forms a mouth, and it speaks in my mother's voice.

"Don't ever touch me again, you freak."

No! I use my power to break it apart. I can't run. I have no legs.

My body. Remember the body before she throws another warped memory at—

It's George Washington University. Yasmine's boyfriend. The first one. He's not breathing. I'm doing CPR and using my powers.

"Don't touch him, you freak!" Yasmine, screaming at me. Not Yasmine. Tamara. Both. I can't tell. "You just want to kill him like you killed my parents! You are evil! All you bring is death! Nothing good comes from your healing! Die!" No! It's a lie, but that doesn't stop it from breaking me inside. These thoughts—mine or Alia's?—they skim too close to reality.

"None of it is real." Tamara. Her voice. In my head. This is all in my head. Everything goes black. I know it's in my head. But I can't get out. Alia's images, they're all so—

Bright light. The savannah. Africa. Nordeen's dreamtime. Great. Now a painful illusion of a fevered, shared sex dream. I'm nauseous. That means something. I can't remember. But I can't be this disorganized. Not with Nordeen in front of me. Only it's not Nordeen. It's Mac. He's the lion-man and Nordeen is the older version of himself. It's an insane fight. Nordeen is using the words of power, whispering down the lion. But Mac is fighting back, taking swipes that barely miss Nordeen. They fight all day, though the sun doesn't move. The fight sounds change. This isn't real . . . this isn't real. I never realized what a pointless statement that is. An explosion happens somewhere . . . In a mind, a power is being used. This means something. It means change. Fuck, another . . .

*

161

Samantha yells at me "You raped me! You're no better than Rajesh!" I know it's not real. She was kind to me. Solace, a place in the storm. Maybe more. This is not an illusion. It's a lie. They're all lies. Work with it. White milk on a sheet. Tuna fish grow gills to protect space from the moon. Come on! I need a good mental hiccup for this girl. Her brain is exploding again. . . .

They're not fighting anymore. Nordeen rides my lion brother's back. They're joined. Heading toward me. Panic. I unleash my powers on them. Nothing happens. I'm running.

"You raped me!"

My brother is a vegetable. This is the one time I visited him in the hospital. It smells of urine and screams silence. He can only make grunting sounds and point with his left hand. He has no power. But when he sees me, his whole body shakes. His bed shakes. But that's all he can do, a short-circuiting of his powers because my fist shoved skull fragments into his brain. I never tried to heal him. There is nothing to make up here. This is all me. How could I even try to be any more than the murderer of my brother?

"Fight back." Tamara. She arrives in the rubble of her own explosion. I feel her fading close by me. Somewhere she's in trouble. Have to figure this out soon.

Getting it. This girl is tap-dancing on my fears, my anxiety, my rage. But none of it is real. So what is it . . . ?

✳

"You would betray me?" Nordeen. He's got me by the throat, dangling over the roof of his house. Fou-Fou and Suleiman wait below with spears and chainsaws. Not real. I know it's not real. But the fear. Face the fear.

"Fuck you. You're not real!"

"You sure about that?" The change is quick. The Dragon Lady. She has me by the throat, hanging me over Soho. No one is noticing. "I can do this all night, little man. You've got no defense. And just so you know, I've decided you're not really worth the effort of keeping. Neither is Tamara. So as I'm killing you, and I'm killing her at the same time."

NO! I kick for the Dragon Lady and find there's nothing there, including a hand to keep me up. And so I fall and land on a spear. It hurts. I look down. A spear is sticking out of my side. I taste the blood. No, I don't. I reach down and my tongue reacts like there's blood. There's no blood.

"Help me, Taggert!" Tamara. Close by. Fully panicked. Almost there, kid. I'm not wounded. I'm not hurt. Not physically. Mentally. She attacks my mind, which is correlated with my brain. My brain is part of my body. I can control my brain.

My lion brother and Nordeen attack again, in unison. Forget the physical danger. What's the emotion? Fear. Old fear. That's my hippocampus. I feel for my own brain, where the bitch has no actual control, and feel it overactive. Chill out. No more old fear.

For a second I can see clearly. Tamara's writhing on the floor, engulfed in flames. Alia sits where we were drinking the sake, smiling. I run towards teh Dragon Lady—

"You raped me!" Hard flash. Samantha again. She's in the car with Mac. They're kissing. In love. Fuck. How many times do I have to live through this same—

Explosion. I'm blown out of the car.

"You raped me." In the car again. This isn't working. This does not traumatize me anymore. All power. No skill. I check my brain again. Amygdala's overworked. Makes sense. My brain's panic button. That was the last time I truly panicked. No more. I'm done with this shit.

The real world returns. I switch my vision from normal to body vision. It helps. Alia doesn't notice me running toward her smug ass. She's too busy torturing Tamara with God only knows what visions. I'm going to start with kicking her in the face. She's sitting in a chair, and I'm going to stomp her face in. I'm going to raise my foot to a level where I'm almost off balance, just to kick her face in. I'm raising my foot but somehow I'm not off balance. But Alia's in the chair and even though I'm this close she doesn't notice. But all I want to do is kick her face in. . . .

Stop!

The illusionist is powerful and subtle. She wants me broken. So she set the illusion up perfectly. Had me thinking I was about to take her out. Instead, I was about to stomp Tamara's pretty little head into so much paste. It's only the thing inside of me that recognizes Tamara almost instinctively that stopped me. It almost worked. Alia almost made me kill Tamara. Yasmine's girl. My—

I hate this Alia bitch. I throw the worst menstrual cramps womankind has ever experienced at Alia and use the time it buys me to try and heal Tamara. I reduce her amygdala and hippocampus as well, but she's like me—still reeling from what she saw. I increase the blood flow to her prefrontal cortex, giving her the gift of reason and long-term planning. Her skin is blistering, just like Rajesh said it would. Psychosomatic illusioning. I tell her body to calm down. To let the burns go. I use my body as a reference point for things like temperature, breathing, and the rest. Her body adapts quicker than I thought possible. But she's still confused, and that's dangerous—too easy to kill me by accident.

"Feel my hand. Listen to my voice, feel my power working through you. Tamara. It's me. It's Taggert. I'm real. All the other stuff was Alia. She got the drop on us. But we're both out of it now. You hear me, girl? It's me. It's Taggert. You tried to push me out of my hotel room. We worked out this plan. It's me. Taggert. Get up off the ground, honey. We've got a fight to finish."

"Daddy?"

"No, it's Taggert."

She looks at me with full recognition and cognizance of what she's saying. "Daddy." I know she's right.

The crowd is confused. The music hasn't stopped, people are still dancing, the flashing lights are still going—but for reasons they can't express, the mood has gotten suddenly colder. Tamara shaking . . . everything going to shit might also have something to do with it.

"I am impressed," Alia says, finally standing in the face of nauseating pain. Tamara and I stand across the street, holding hands, sweaty and sure. This bitch is dead. She just doesn't know it yet. "No one's ever broken one of my illusions before."

"Shouldn't try and keep two people like us down at once," I say. I think to Tamara *Blow out all the video screens and cameras.* She does, with the exactitude of someone well accustomed to using their powers.

"Last chance for you to join up with me." There. I heard it. A little bit of fear in her voice.

"Go to hell, you murderous cunt!" Tamara barks but doesn't move. We're in telepathic communication now. Fully. No need to hide it. We're both the stronger for it. I'll heal the strain the use of all this power puts on her fourteen-year-old body. She cedes the direction of her powers to me.

"Just remember, I tried to give you a way out." Alia closes her eyes. Tamara braces for a direct attack on us, but I know how this bitch thinks now. "They're demons. Attack the demons." She's not talking to us. She's talking to everyone else here.

We're in a crowd of at least a thousand, and they all want us dead. Before anyone can move, now that I have a lock on Alia I cause muscle death in both of her legs. I hear her cry of pain and know she's not going anywhere. I was hoping it would chill out the crowd, too. Nope, they're just angry Londoners with faces painted like samurai, some with real swords, ready for a fight.

"Got an idea," Tamara says, gripping my hand hard.

"I'm not trying to kill all these people."

"Me neither. But I think its nap time."

"All these people at once?"

"Remember the pebble, grasshopper," she says, with all the humor she can muster after just dodging a sword stroke. We join minds again and send out a wave of need for sleep—the physical depletion comes from me, with a psychic nudge from Tamara. We can only do about fifty at a time, so we do the closest fifty. Their slumbering bodies block any dangerous people behind them. We're like radiation, invisible, powerful, deadly. Get close enough to us, and you start to suffer from radiation sleeping sickness. Yet we're demons who have to be slaughtered, if the voices in your head are to be believed. These poor norms are caught between two sets of powers. They're lucky we're just making them sleep. A few minutes later and even the DJ's and local store clerks are out.

The only one awake is Alia. She's managed to crawl into a bar, and she's downing large amounts of whiskey from the bottle. Her illusions are gone, and I finally get to see her real face. She can't be more than ten years old. That's why Tamara's darts didn't work. They were aimed too high. She's barely four foot. And she's ugly. Not everyday ugly—she had major genetic problems: oversized cranium, malformed palette, cleft lip—mother-was-probably-her-sister-type ugly. Her teeth are gray and look like they belong to an infant. Her arms are deformed, almost flippers. Her knees can't handle the weight of her thighs, so they buckle constantly. Her organs are too large for her rib cage so they press against skin that's so translucent, you can see veins everywhere. She's got to have some extra sensory ability just to get around because those eyes can't focus together. It looks like she tried to grow a second nose by her right temple, but it just ended up as a cancerous-looking growth. She breathes in a hiss. I couldn't do this to someone on my most vindictive day.

"Don't you look at me like that." Can't figure out who she's talking to, me or Tamara. Tamara has her hand over her mouth and seems to feel genuine pity. Something that, even without the illusion, I just can't seem to muster.

"Don't you look at me like I'm some sort of freak," she says. I'm not sure if she's slurring her words because of the liquor, or if that's just the way she talks. "You are just like me. Just like me."

Tamara has more courage than I do. She sits across a table from the thing that just invaded our minds and tried to kill us. She doesn't say anything, though, just stares. Alia tries to raise her powers against her, but Tamara does something with a wave of her hand that makes Alia wince. The creature breathes hard before speaking again.

"See, you're like me. A freak. Only difference is, you're a pretty freak."

"So you say, yeah?" Tamara says, giving up some sightless fight.

"Don't do that," the thing hisses.

"What?"

"The patronizing. You won, yeah. But don't patronize. I deserve more than that. I made it big, get me? Me and Prentis made . . ."

She takes a drink. I stand behind my girl, looking down at the thing. "Me and Prentis. We were like sisters growing up. Ran away from the group home together. Prentis was older. She knew the street. Everybody knew her. She had the dogs and cats and rats and birds. And they all loved her. And she made them love me, too. No people did. I learned to read when I was one. I could talk by two. By three I could write. I was special. No one cared. All they saw was that I was ugly. But Prentis cared. She took care of me. I wasn't getting adopted. That much was clear. So when she ran, I went with her. Lived underground with her."

"Then your powers kicked in," I say. I reach for her bottle. She hands it over, curious. When I don't wipe the top off before I take a swig, I can feel a little happiness in her. I'm so conflicted I don't know what to do with that.

"Yeah, and with the powers I became pretty. I was pretty and sexy and smart. I could do whatever I wanted." I think it's smiling.

"Then why do you treat Prentis that way?" Tamara has a tear in her eye. Only one. I think she's just about cried out.

"Because she's not smart!" the thing hisses, demanding its bottle back. "And she's ugly. I tried to give her new clothes—she says she doesn't want them because they're stolen. I tried to give her men, women, whatever she wanted. She said she only wanted us to be good friends—together again. She's limited. Same with Rajesh. I don't care that you killed him. He was strong, but nothing else. No smarts. No one is as smart as me. Not even you two. Just lucky is all."

"Not lucky, yeah?" Tamara says. "Loved. Had someone who had my back in the name of my mom, yeah? That's all you ever wanted, ennit? It's not my power, not my skill. Wanted my life, you did. That's why you took my parents out. Didn't want me to have anyone else, just like you."

If it's crying, then it's the most unattractive crying sound I've ever heard in my life. Alia sighs big and deep, like she has three lungs instead of two. Shit, maybe she does. I don't want to know.

Snot pours from her nose and mouth. Green gunk from her eyes. I'm caught between wanting to heal her and being repulsed by the idea of touching that skin.

"It's not fair." Alia whines. "Why couldn't I have a family? When . . . when I reached out for others, like Nordeen, that was all I wanted . . . family. But no one responded. I knew you were a setup from the beginning, healer. I knew that. But I had to take the chance, didn't I? Had to know if someone actually reached back to me. Why didn't anyone reach back to me? Is it because I'm ugly? Do they know I'm ugly in Africa?"

I walk over to the other side of the booth and sit next to her. I take another swig from the bottle. I offer it to Tamara, after making sure none of fluids on it contain anything contagious. She takes a swig as well. Then I speak. "No one knows what you look like. Nobody responded because you were too powerful to be a good servant and too smart to be a mere ally. All of this was just a matter of time."

"So no one could have ever loved me?" It's so pathetic I feel my rage slipping. Same can't be said for Tamara.

"Someone did love you. She loved you and gave you everything she had. She gave you everything you ever wanted. And in return you felt disgust for her compassion. You called it weakness. You tried to break her, and all she did was give you opportunity after opportunity to do something right. For someone so smart, you are an idiot." Tamara stands from the booth. Alia's as smart as she claims. She senses what's coming next.

"I have money!" Alia says, grabbing Tamara's arm. "Accounts. I played the American stock market. Japanese, too. I have money. Plus the revenue from the parties. Let's take it and go somewhere. I'll get better, I promise. No more killings."

"Shh." Tamara's got her agitated face on. She holds the thing's hands on her arms. "The dumbest thing about you is that you didn't realize how close all the things you ever wanted were to you. Taggert, heal her." I lay my hands on her while Tamara holds her tight. It's a chore. It's deficient RNA strands and chromosomal damage. Alia is a true mutation. Most people like us have physiologies that mimic normal human types easily. Alia's got organs I can't even identify. Her blood doesn't match anything I've ever seen. It's so oxygenated I doubt she really needed to breathe. In some ways she's a highly adapted creature. It's only the external features that are warped. She wasn't designed for life on this planet. Maybe that's why her power allowed her to shape her surroundings so completely. I do the work asked of me and add one caveat of my own. I destroy the pickle-sized organ in her brain that rested where her amygdala should've been. That was how she was able to create the images.

For those sleeping outside it would have been her physical trans-formation that was most striking. I give her height, strengthening her leg muscles and replacing the reverse buckling growths at the midpoint of her legs with proper knees. I perform ten thousand dol-lars' worth of dental work in about a minute, reforming her palette, dropping out her excess teeth and forcing some of them to retreat back into the gums. Then I have to stop the gums from bleeding and oozing whatever that black liquid is. I drop all the webbing between her fingers, toes, forearms and pits, and smooth the hide-like patches of skin at the top of her head and the back of her neck with thin delicate skin. I reduce her cranium gently and reshape it to make it look more . . . human. I utilize the excess mass of her extra organs to metabolize the cellulite, bone, nerves, and other stray biological material that rested in her chest cavity. She is by no means perfect when I'm done, but I have a newfound respect for what it takes for a liminal person to look human. When I'm done, I'm all but spent. Alia gets up, stretches her legs for the first time, and understands what balance is. Tamara moves close to me. Props me up. I'm sweating.

"You okay, Taggert?"

"Fine. You okay?"

"Will be in a second."

Alia spins like a ten-year-old girl with a dress on. She jumps. She touches the fully formed teeth in her mouth, her lip. She smoothes back her ratty red mane. She giggles and tries out her voice, saying her own name over and over again. She's four years younger than Tamara, but she's acting like a three-year-old. She stands in front of a mirror looking at her legs. I wonder if she sees Tamara walk up behind her. I'm passive in this one.

I'll back either play Tamara makes. To pity Alia means to live a life taking care of her, watching her, managing her. She's an abused animal that needs lots of clean living and distance, a life far from anyone she could hurt. She's also a predator who is a master manipulator at age ten. I understand why Nordeen sent me against our kind so often now. Without some kind of containment, our kind can split the skies, or at the very least split the souls of humanity. Alia is living proof. Tamara knows all this, I can still feel our latent telepathic connection. I sense her giddiness at making Alia happy combine with a rage that's burned so hard for three days that it almost has a name of its own, a face. I can see Tamara's power, the thing inside of her, and it is angry. I can still hear the smile in Alia's voice.

"Does this mean we can be friends now?" Tamara is surprisingly quick with a sword. Alia never felt it coming.

Chapter Sixteen

It's almost a full day before our psychic connection fades to the point where we have to speak again. Neither one of us tries to reestablish it, both happy to have some alone time in our own craniums. When we do speak, it's in a cab headed toward a townhouse in Crystal Palace.

"He can find you even in Bromley." We both know who she's talking about.

"I know," I say, taking in the landscape.

"So why not go find him? Let me plead your case."

"Girl, there's nothing you can say he hasn't already heard. You show up in front of him, and all the hard work I've done to keep you a secret goes out the window. What good is that then, huh?"

"Not like you to be scared of a man," she snipes coldly.

"Not sure he is one, love."

After a minute Tamara throws herself under my arm.

"It's not like you could stop me if I was committed." Truer words were never spoken. She's powerful. More than powerful now she's learning how to be subtle. She grabbed all the finance codes from Alia's head before she decapitated her. Now she's got the cash. Alia was right—neither one of us are as smart she was. In two years she turned five thousand quid into two point three million euros. I told Tamara it would keep her well fit. She said it'd keep us just as secure.

But money wasn't the issue. And strangely enough, neither was Nordeen.

"My name is Tamara Bridgecombe," she says in her old accent. The accent of her prep school, where she belongs. It's three days after what people are calling the "most bizarre Bender party" ever. Police are still trying to make sense of the decapitated little girl that no one seemed to know in a pub in Soho. Fingerprints, dental records, photos are all coming up blank on the girl. The mass nap is being attributed to a gas leak. No one has any theories about the massive screens all failing at the same time.

The townhouse we're staying in is from my pre-Nordeen days, as is the owner. He was happy to hear my voice, and happy for the next five mortage payments I give him to rent his little slice of heaven.

"I know your name," I say, closing the house laptop. Tamara looks over from the couch she's been recuperating on. She found a white knit sweater, stretched long and wide enough to fit two of her in a closet. She hasn't taken it off since we settled in. It suits her, and reminds me she's a child.

I haven't asked her about killing Alia. Haven't asked her about her parents. Haven't asked her about much, really. But every night she sleeps in my bed, and I sit watch for her. Halfway through she'll start sobbing, low and consistent. Occasionally a word or two will slip in. "Mommy." "Daddy." "I'm sorry." She's usually up early, five at the latest. She reads a lot. Takes walks. Thinks.

"What I mean is, my father is Darren Bridgecombe." I nod. I've never been a father to anyone. I wouldn't know how. "But I know that you loved my mother. And I know that she loved you. And when I was all alone, you stood by me. And I know that your blood is in me. So what does that make you to me?"

"Friend. Confidant. Someone that will never do anything intentionally or unintentionally to hurt you."

"Not good enough," she says, getting on her knees on the couch so she can look at me properly across the room.

"What are you talking about?"

"So you'll never do anything intentionally or unintentionally to hurt me. What about protect me? Alia had me dead to rights, yeah? If it wasn't for you, I'd be dead. You said it yourself—she was a novice. What if one your biggies come? Someone with skill and power? Where am I then? Someone's cup of tea is what I am. Somebody's buttered toast to snack on."

"You're getting smarter with your power every day—"

"Sell it to someone else, Taggert. You and I both know I need more training if I'm not going to end up a bigger fish's meal."

"I'm not taking you over to him."

"Good. Tag, you've got to have sex with a stranger in order to talk to him. I do not want to meet such a man. I want you to stay here, with me."

"I stay, he comes, we both die."

"You sure on that, mate? 'Cause from what you told me, Alia said—"

"Not the most reliable of sources," I point out.

"Not on her own, but didn't your little sex conduit said something similar about him? Shit, even the man himself told you things he didn't quite understand were going on here in London. Plus, by your own account, Nord—"

"Don't say his name." I've been like this since all of Alia's visions. He's been a plague to me. All the paternal feeling I've had for him has disappeared, leaving just a big ball of confusion where my chest should be.

"OK. But even you said he hasn't left Morocco in years. What do you think would get him over here?"

"You," I say sharply. I get up and cross the room to sit next to her. The sun is rising slowly. As streaks of light come through the French doors, the birdbath in the enclosed garden outside comes to life. "At fourteen, you've survived more than most of our kind ever will. Most of us live like your mom did. I loved her, but she was ashamed and embarrassed by her powers. That's most of us. Some of us, like Alia, like my brother, go mad with the power and usually end up breaking themselves or someone else beyond repair. But you, you're street-smart and getting more skilled every day. You are a jewel. Do you get that? If anyone is out there collecting people like us then you're the top on their list. If my boss finds out about you—"

"Then you'd fight him, right?" She still has the shocked eyes, the thousand-yard stare of a little body that's seen too much. "If he ever came for me, now or in fifty years, you'd stand by my side, right?"

"Don't ask questions you already know the answer to."

"So why wait? Stand with me now. You say he knows about everything anyway. Sooner or later he'll come for me, if I'm the treasure you claim I am. So why go back? To delay the inevitable? Why not take the time to teach me so that maybe, just maybe, I can stand up to him on my own?"

"It's not that simple!"

"But it is. You've been a slave to that razor around your neck for too long, Taggert. You shouldn't fear saying his name—he should fear saying yours. Before you didn't have anything to fight for. Now you do. You aren't my dad, but you are my father. Fight for me. Stay for me."

I am quiet that whole day, and tell her I'm going out that night. She gives me a look, then decides it's OK to trust me. Still not used to being trusted. I get on the tube and pick up a paper. Official ruling from Scotland Yard came in. Tamara's listed as a runaway. Given that her passport was missing from her room, it's assumed she's gone abroad. They're already painting her as a spoiled brat who had the best of everything and wouldn't even come home for her parents' funeral. Leave it to the dailies to get it all wrong.

In the oddities section there's a report of an Indian restaurant using a rancid ghee that was so toxic it caused all the patrons to vomit and led to a fatal allergic reaction in the son of the owners. The Indian couple that owns the restaurant says they are moving back to Bangalore.

I get off the train but stay on the platform until it's relatively empty. I give everyone a bright flash in their eyes with my power and then jump on the tracks. I follow the path Tamara blazed for me what seems like ages ago. Halfway there and I can feel a familiar heartbeat. She doesn't have the raw strength to move cement blocks, so Prentis had the rats burrow a nice-sized hole for her. It *is* her old apartment after all. She's got a right to be here.

When I go in I find more animals than I thought possible huddled behind, around, and under her. The rats, cats, and dogs are all remarkably quiet. The pigeons and smaller birds can't seem to help their squawking. None of them attack. All of them are quaking in fear of the big bad man. Me.

"I'm trying to send them away!" she begs. "I am. Please don't kill them. I'll do whatever you want. Please, just don't kill them." Then she snaps. "You kill them, you better kill me first. I'll send them all, every dog, cat, insect. I'll send them all after you." My first assessment of her was right. She's not a soldier. Trained troops don't announce winning strategies. Nordeen is right to want her. A day in his care, and she would be unbeatable.

I take a seat on the bed, unbutton the deep red peacoat my friend with the townhouse left for me. I take her in for a second. All of her. Then I speak.

"Why won't they leave?" I ask, genuinely curious.

"They . . . they know what you did to the others. They know what you want to do to me."

I nod my head in agreement and think before I speak. "About the others, the dogs and rats when we first met. I'm sorry. I didn't know they were your friends." One of the dogs, a pearl-eyed border collie who was silently baring his teeth, stops snarling but keeps his tail rigged in the air.

"You can leave," Prentis offers. I'm a little confused. "I mean, if you leave, I'll leave. I'll go to a new county maybe? Like France? Is that OK? Someplace else. I won't tell about Rajesh or Alia. I swear, I can—"

"I don't want to hurt you." The dog bares his teeth again, and the whole mass of animals trembles, pulling in even closer. I realize what an implicit threat I've made. "I won't hurt you."

It takes Prentis a long time to ask the question we both have. "Why?"

"Me and you, little girl. We're a lot alike. No family. No friends. Not a lot of people knowing what we can really do. Those that do know want to use us, as if we were wrenches or hammers or something, you know? Me and you, we don't really know any better way. We've been used our whole lives. I don't want to speak for you, but sometimes I really believe that if I don't have someone telling me what to do, telling me what they want and need, then I wouldn't know what to do with my time."

"Animals." She says it just a little larger than a whisper. "The animals, what they do with their time is simple. Find food, sleep, poop, play. That's it. That's the day-to-day. I like that world. People are different."

"Are we though, Prentis? Are we that different? Because to be honest, all I want is to take a good rest when I'm tired, let go of bad things that build up in me, and enjoy myself. That's all I want. I just never thought that was possible."

"I didn't mean to bring Tamara into all this trouble."

"I know. She knows. You were trapped." She nods a little. A small dog, a black puppy with way too much baby fur, leaves her side and comes to mine. He sniffs a lot. I don't pet him. "You do that?"

"No. I mean, kind of. It's not like on the telly with the superheroes, you know? Where they, like, have all this control and the animals do what they say. These are my friends. If I've got questions, they want to know the answers. Someone's attacking me, they want to protect me."

"So I should take this pup as you being curious about me?" She shrugs her shoulders, revealing a massive python resting behind her. "Fair enough. So let me just say this, then. I'm sorry for killing your animal friends before. I didn't realize what was going on."

"It's all right," she says, wiping the tears from her face. "My fault really. Putting them in harm's way and all. I had asked them to do a lot before. Most of it they didn't understand. Never asked them to go to their deaths. Didn't think they'd do it. Figured they'd run away after you did . . . whatever it was you did to them. But they kept fighting for me. Even when I told them not to. I told them all to get away from you, but they wouldn't hear it. They was all, even this lot, everyone, willing to die for me. How's a body supposed to handle that?"

I give her a completely honest shrug.

Looking around the station (turned liminal girl flop), I realize who I'm sitting in front of. All the decorations belong to Prentis. This hardened street child, this liminal one, is a typical teenage girl complete with impossible crushes and fantasy loves. "It's been a crazy week and a half for me, Prentis. Maybe you, too?"

"Heard you killed Alia." I nod, opting out of specifics. "Rajesh, too?" She shakes when she says his name.

"Both of them are gone."

"I understand about Alia. She wasn't all bad."

"I know."

"Just the runt of the litter, yeah? Didn't like always being looked down upon, is all. Tried to look out for her. Tried to be her friend. But she wasn't hearing me, always trying to fiddle with things. . . . You probably think she didn't like me, right? Wrong. She loved me, like a sister, like a mother. See, but she couldn't understand how to show it, thought it was a limitation to love somebody."

"It was quick." She nods. Before she asks, I tell her. "I took my time with Rajesh." She's smiling. More animals lounge between the two of us.

"You here for me, then?" she asks. "Want me to work for you, like I did for Alia?"

"Not so much, no. I want to try something new. See if you're up for it. If not, I swear you'll be left in peace—at least by me. See, Tamara's got this idea that she and I should live together. I'd train her, give her lessons, learn her proper in case a bigger, badder Alia came around. I'm thinking if I do it for one, I could do it for two."

She blinks more times than I thought possible . She tries to speak, coughs. Tries again.

"I killed her mum and dad."

"No, you didn't."

"I swear I did. Alia she said she wanted me to keep tabs on them, so I asked the rats to keep a look out for their scent and they found them and then Rajesh he blew them up. You see? I'm responsible. I couldn't, I can't look her in the eye."

"But when she took up refuge here, the rats knew. That means you knew. But you didn't tell."

She nods. "Penance after the car blew up. I wasn't in favor of the killings, yeah? But still, I can't . . ." Again I nod. Then I breathe deep and tell her some truth.

"I killed my brother," I tell her. She pulls her head back slightly. "He was like us. Had powers like Tamara. I punched his head in until all I saw was red."

"Was he a bad man?"

"Was Alia a bad girl? My brother had the same problem she did. Didn't know what to do with someone that loved them too much. Is that bad? You tell me. That's not the point. Point is I did something that I considered unforgivable. Didn't help that no one around me would forgive me, either. I never tried to make amends. I never tried to make it right. I just assumed that if I did it once, then that's what I was, that was all I was destined to be. I spent years trying to heal people, trying to make that right wrong, never realizing that's what I was doing. I don't wish that on you. I don't wish that on anyone. Did you mess up? Of course you did. And our kind tends to mess up big. My question is, when are you going to start trying to rectify your mistakes?

"Who are we to make such mistakes and ask to be forgiven?

"Someone called us liminal people. It's the best description I've heard yet. We dance the line between humans and gods. Some of us think they're too much like gods. I'd like to see what it feels like to be human. Humans have families. Maybe the ones we're born into, but how about the ones we choose?"

"She can't forgive me," Prentis states.

"Yeah? 'Cause if she does it'll mean you'll have to be in charge of your own life? You'll have to live a human life. No more living underground. No more dumpster diving for food. If she forgives you, it means you have to enter the real world and try to make some sense of it. I know from experience, the life of a slave can be easier than the life of a human. But don't get it twisted. You can only be one or the other. A human being or a slave." I stand, and for the first time since I put it on, I take the razor-blade necklace off.

"This is my chain, Prentis. My master made all his servants wear them to let us know how close we were to death. He likes to joke that if god is as close to you as your jugular vein, then he is even closer. Stupid joke with no humor, you know? I'm tired of being a slave, Prentis. Aren't you?"

She stands for the first time, and all the animals flow off of her like water. In her own dirty way, she's gentle and kind with them all. She can't weigh more than eighty-five pounds. Her face is pockmarked, and her dirty blond hair is oily and reeks of garbage. Her clothes are two sizes too big for her. But she smiles, and she looks glorious to me. I drop the razor and like magic I feel lighter.

✳

I give Prentis a one hundred euro note and the address where Tamara is staying. She's cautiously optimistic entering the cab. I don't blame her. A couple of days ago this would have been a scam I would have used to deliver her to Nordeen. Now, it's a genuine act of kindness so foreign to my character I'm questioning whether I'm actually doing it. I'm about to call Tamara when her quixotic voice enters my mind. "Good job," I feel her say. I also feel her restraint in not calling me father. I wonder whose benefit it's for. I go white milk on white sheets in my mind, before I think anymore.

My conversation with the animal girl opened a possibility so simple that it had eluded me for the past thirteen years. A possibility that, if true, makes life infinitely more complicated in the long term—but easier to manage in the short. I look up in the sky and see a beneficent alien descending on the streets of London. I think they call it the sun. I take it as a good omen, a sunny day in London.

The familiar flood of pheromones is so comforting I take a full few minutes in front of Samantha's door before I regulate my body to be as immune as possible. She opens with a grin before I'm done knocking.

I took my time getting to her neighborhood again, not out of fear, just judging all the angles on the next most important conversation I'll ever have. I watched a movie and ate a great dinner. I went to the bridge where Yasmine died and said a silent prayer to my own ambiguous gods, asking that her soul be kept safe . . . and close to Fish'n'Chips, a better husband and father than I ever managed to be. I told her to keep an eye out for me, because I might be seeing her soon. Ten times during the day and night I felt the tickle in the back of my mind—Tamara, trying to talk to me. But I sensed no urgency in her, no danger. She just wanted to know where I was. Sorry, luv, if this works out you can have me for the rest of my life, but this thing I have to do on my own.

"I'm sorry, I know it's late," I offer as Samantha opens her door, this time in a red wrap. It's two in the morning and she's smoking that sweet smelling not-pot again.

"I welcome you into my house, Taggert." It's a formality. As soon as I step in, she hugs me hard and blows some of that smoke into my mouth. It's a bliss-filled intoxicant ride that even my regulatory powers can't shake off. "I'm so happy you made it through your journey alive."

"As am I. I want to thank you for what you gave me."

"And you'd like to ask me if I'd be willing to do it again."

"But your opinion first. If you're willing."

"I will make tea. You will sit. Then we will speak."

I wait until she's ready, and I lay it out for her. I don't hold anything back. Not just about the past week or so. But my entire life. From Mac to Yasmine, to London the first time, the relief work, the Mog, the trek, the Dogon, Nordeen, the Aussie, South Africa, the lie I got away with the last time I was here. What I did to Rajesh, what Tamara did to Alia, every detail I can I tell her. I trust her. I shouldn't. I don't know her. But I'm trying new things, so I end with what I consider to be the most valuable piece of information.

She listens with the patience of a priestess. Her questions are only probing in that they get me to speak more. She watches me except for when I tell her about killing the liminal children. And though she doesn't look at me, I know it's not out of judgment , but because she knows I'm unaccustomed to such honesty. All she does is listen. I respect her for it. Love her for it. I describe some of the darkest bits of my history, my soul, and her implacable face doesn't change. When I'm done she pours more chocolate tea. We drink in silence.

"I was taught a name," she says. "It's a name in a dead tongue, and so it has power. It is the name of the first growing sentience on this planet. It is the name of the first of the old gods. It was the god that was consumed by the other gods, the god which gave them the sustenance they needed to go on creating the rest of the universe. The home of that eaten god is Earth, and it is from that god that all other deities have sprung. To say its name in the presence of some causes great pain. In others it is a source of great relief."

"Samantha, I appreciate your religion but—"

"I've told you this before, Taggert. This is not religion, this is fact." She rises to her knees and leans over in my ear. "I give you this name, healer, so that if you have nothing else you may call on my god to protect you." And she says the name. Like the words Nordeen used to reduce the lion, this word is weighted. But I am not heavier for hearing it. Instead, I am aware of my own contribution to the weight of the world. I want to speak it.

"Hold it close to your heart now," she says, leaning back into her seat. "Just as a scalpel can be a weapon, it can also be an instrument of healing. Intent is important with names such as this."

"Why . . . why did you tell me your god's name?"

"From the time you left, I've been petitioning my . . . congregation for permission to do so. I know of no greater strength to offer. I told you so that it might help in your coming conversation with your former master. And because I was directed to by mine. Can we go to bed now?"

"Where is your razor?" It's the younger Nordeen I face. But we are not in the jungle. We are sitting at a table on my rooftop in Biya. A place I will most likely never see again.

"I will not be wearing it anymore, Nordeen." A harsh snort, a mix of a laugh and a grunt, escapes his spirit mouth.

"It seems the Ethiope bitch has limited my abilities in this visit. My goal was to devour your head whole."

"I didn't think anyone had the power to curtail you." I pour spirit tea for him and offer it. It's the first time I've seen confusion in the old man's face. He turns to the illusory sea.

"In this medium, as it is only spirit stuff, your whore—"

"I'd appreciate it if you'd stop calling her that," I bark.

"It's pheromones, you addlepated oaf!" he barks back. "The only reason I sent you to her is because I thought you'd be able to defend yourself against them."

"I have. This isn't about her."

"Are you sure? Don't say it's about religion. Don't tell me she's converted you to her heretical ravings. . . ."

"It's not about the religion, either. I didn't like, don't like, who I am under your control."

"But you are powerful with me." He turns to face me. "Think on it, Taggert. Could you truly have asked for a better teacher than I? Not only opportunity and time to study your skill, but you also had interactions with others like us. Who else could have given you that?"

"And it is for that reason I'm meeting with you now. I would be a liar if I said I didn't appreciate what you've done for me. But the price is too high."

"What price, boy? What have I made you do—?"

"You made me kill children!"

"Psychotic children that should've never been born. Twisted approximations of us at best, bastard spawn of demigods at worst. My God, Taggert, do you truly view me as such a monster that I would order the random slaying of children?"

"Yes." It seems his fury will explode from his skin for a minute, and then he smiles.

"Of course I would. It's good to know you've grown past me bluffing you. By the way, when you wake tell your whore that she, as well as you, your daughter, and the totem girl are officially on my list. And when I come to London—"

"You come to London and all the tricks I've ever learned, seen, thought about, imagined, had nightmares of, and fantasized about will be leveled against you and whatever powers you bring." I'm furious. He knows about Tamara. "I was yours. I did as you asked, without question, for seven years. My time serving you is over."

"But you will serve someone, Taggert. If not me, then one of my allies. And if not them, then one of my enemies. But make no mistake, little healer, you cannot remain neutral in the forthcoming battle. I know you. I know your secret desires. Like the stupid

American you are, you would try and take the Ethiopian as a wife and raise the totem girl and your daughter as sisters. Where do you think a quartet of power like that will be able to hide, boy?"

"If I have to serve, it won't be you!"

"Again I ask you, this time in all seriousness, what was so wrong with serving me? You killed children? So what? Do you know how many children there are on this planet? One more or less doesn't make any difference to anyone. The stakes that are coming will make one human life the equivalent of a peanut in a bag. Life, human life, our individual lives, do not matter."

"Another might believe that, Nordeen. But I am a healer. Despite what you may think of me, I am at my heart a healer. All life matters."

"Does life matter so much that the illusionist is still alive? How about her friend, who killed your old flame? Is he still alive? Or were you thankful for the opportunity to cull them both, as I knew you would be when I sent you up there?"

"What?" Even in my spirit body I'm shaken.

He clucks his sprit tongue and looks out at the sea. I think it's real until he waves his hand and turns the waters red. "You know better than almost any other living being on the planet how easily I could turn this image into reality. I could drown the coast of England in blood and muck and mire. You cry about the children I've had you dispatch. Imagine what one with my age and their temperament could do. Name me evil if it helps you sleep better, Taggert, but know that I've been practicing Atlas-like levels of restraint since before your country of origin was even formed. What you call evil, I call the bigger picture. I knew you'd go to London. My goal was for you to bring all four of the young ones under your wing—and by extension under mine. But what was I to tell you? That your former lover and your bastard child had need of you? That it was better for them to be protected by the legend of my power than some flimsy junior politician? Think, boy—what other reason did I have for letting you keep the necklace on? I sent you out in the hope that you would bring more of us back. But as luck would have it, this Alia child was too deranged and your daughter too resourceful. Fine. You still managed to bond both the whelps to you. Beg forgiveness, here and now, and I won't go to my contingency plans. Come now, Taggert, think. When do I ever lose? I wouldn't send you off to foreign lands without having a way of getting you back in line, would I?" It takes me a second. I'm afraid, more afraid than I've ever been in my life. He could have my brother, fully healed, waiting in the wings. Samantha could be one of his. That's how devious he is. Tamara, Prentis, they could have already been under his control before I even got here. But I will be brave.

"Yes, you would send me," I say quickly. "You'd send me because you love me." He stands, knocking over the table.

"What . . . ?" And I see it. The chink in the mighty Nordeen armor. "You've gone mad."

"Maybe. But why else would you send me out to collect the one thing you couldn't give me, a family? It was the kindness of your nature, such as it is."

"I've encouraged you to breed!"

"I said a *family*." I stay seated, remembering that I am safe in a glass bed next to a woman capable of stopping this interaction if it becomes too untenable. "Yes, you've pushed whores and norms my way. But another one like us? Never. You say you knew about Tamara. That means you've known about her for a while. But you found a way to send me to her when she needed me most. I know how your mind works, Nordeen. You wanted to frame me as the hero so the girl and her mother would look to me for support. No doubt you had a plan to get rid of Bridgecombe, leaving me the inherited parent."

"You are a competent parrot, boy. I've said as much already."

"True, but not the why of it. There are a thousand and one ways you could have gotten both of them to come to you. A simple alliance with Alia would have gotten at least *her* under your wing, maybe . . . maybe even saved Yasmine's life. It wasn't their powers you wanted. It was them. And it wasn't for you personally. It was for me. You did what you could to give me a family so that I would stay with you, love you like you love—"

"Has your time in London limited your scope of vision so severely that you can't see the difference between control and love?" His rage radiates, turning not only the sea but also the sky red. But my table, my tea, and my mind stay the passive blue that I will always associate with the good times in Biya. "When I brought you to Suleiman, did you think I didn't know his wife was having a hard time conceiving? Do you think I didn't know he would love you for your minimal efforts and hence ease your transaction into the razor-necks? Do you think I don't know how he still watches, forever concerned that you might take his position as my right-hand man? And do you think I don't know how you do the same with him?"

"I know how you used me, Nordeen," I say, borrowing the technique Samantha taught me of speaking without judgment. "But I think in this one case, you didn't realize how affected you would be by your tool. I know you started off wanting me to be your dog, your slave. But I think you've come to love me." His gaze is intense. I have never seen him so enraged. But when I'm done with my cup of tea, I pour him another—and watch as once more he is utterly confused.

"So be it." He begins to walk away. "May your delusion dissipate enough for you to be a worthy opponent by the time my principals and powers come to fetch you and yours."

"Thank you."

"What? Child . . ." He stops, realizing the implication of his word choice. "I am declaring unholy war on you and yours."

"I know. But before the mayhem begins I just want to thank you, while I still can. For all that you gave me, all that you showed me, Nordeen. For your love. You've been more than a father to me than my own blood. You're right. I wouldn't have gotten the exposure to so much if it hadn't been for you. I wish we could part under better terms. I didn't come here for us to fight. I came so that I could tell you that I appreciated what you did for me. Most of it, anyway."

"You will not stay my hand with this sentimental—"

"There's no ploy in this, old man. I am actually not your enemy. I just no longer wish to be under your wing. You have to know what that feels like, to want to strike out on your own." With spirit eyes, I close the distance between his yellow orbs and mine, and for a second I see nothing but questioning. I realize then he does not know what it means to be your own individual. He has always served someone else.

"Stay out of Africa, Taggert!" He walks down spirit steps to the spirit beach as it slowly compromises between his violent crimson and my passive blues. As he gains distance, I still hear him clearly. "Tell your whore the next time she sees me she'd better have the protection of her god firmly established. Guard your children like a hawk and raise them well. If they wash up upon any of my beaches, they will not be returned."

I wake up. The day is new. Samantha wraps her powerful thighs around me. Her scent is intoxicating. But responsibility calls already. I've left the girls alone overnight. I call them. They're making waffles. Tamara quips, "If the first shag is for secure contact, what's the second time for?" I tell her I quit. She says so there's no need for more sex. I hang up.

"Who was that?" the miniature Ethiopian goddess asks.

"My daughter." We both smile at the sound of that. "I don't think she likes you."

"It is not uncommon for a girl to be jealous of her father's . . . paramours." I nod. Over chocolate tea I tell Samantha about the entire conversation with Nordeen.

"You were wrong about one thing," I mention softly.

"Only one?" She smiles, showing me brilliant teeth.

"Nordeen did protect me. He showed me the world. This world, our world."

"There are better ways," she starts.

"But that was his way. Look, I'm not saying I'll do the same for the girls, but when I had to get Tamara ready to fight, I trained her in hours. If not for Nordeen, I never would have been able to."

Samantha stands from her table and finds one of her special-blend joints to smoke.

"There is more to this world than fighting."

"I agree, but—"

"Then let us be happy that we agree on that, if nothing else," she says, lighting her joint. Her inhale is deep.

"I've offended you."

"Oh no, dear healer. Not at all. If I seemed distracted just now it's because I've received a message from the herald of the new god." She smiles and exhales an impossibly large puff. The smoke acts as a living thing, forsaking the rest of the world and circling my body.

"You've lost me."

"Never." She winks. "I think I am supposed to meet your daughters."

"Tamara is my only . . ." And then I stop, realizing Nordeen made the same "mistake." Biologically, Prentis is not my child, but if anyone knows how mutable and ultimately inconsequential biology is, it's me. What matters is family. Alia was willing to rip London in two to make Tamara part of hers, and Tamara bisected herself—one part teenage girl, the other liminal killing machine—to avenge hers. Prentis would have been happy with her animal family had Alia not screwed it up. Samantha speaks of her religion as though it's the ultimate family. Even Nordeen scoured the world, probably for centuries on end, trying to make sure his "family" was controllable. His only weakness was his love for me, his "son."

I'm the only one who'd given up on family. Maybe it was Mac, my mother, maybe even Yasmine, but somewhere along the line I'd simply allowed the dream of being in a stable and supportive community to collapse around me. Yet somehow, through no conscious effort of my own, I now have two "daughters" to care for, and a gorgeous Ethiopian woman who seems determined to join us for waffles at least.

Nordeen is right. There is no way we can all stay under the radar in the coming storms. That's the one thing he and Samantha seem to agree on. But I know that whatever comes, we'll all be able to weather it better together than apart.

About the Author

Ayize Jama-Everett was born in 1974 and raised in Harlem, New York. Since then he has traveled extensively in Northern Africa, New Hampshire, and Northern California. He holds a Master's in Clinical Psychology and a Master's in Divinity. He teaches religion and psychology at Starr King School for the Ministry when he's not working as a school therapist at the College Preparatory School. When not educating, studying, or beating himself up for not writing enough, he's usually enjoying aged rums and practicing his aim.

31901056703558